ÆSOP'S FABLES

Angela K Bryant

IIA

" The birds all set off for the castle of King Eagle."

Frontispiece.

ÆSOP'S FABLES

RETOLD BY

BLANCHE WINDER

WITH 48 COLOUR PLATES
BY

HARRY ROUNTREE

WARD, LOCK & CO., LIMITED
LONDON AND MELBOURNE

MADE IN ENGLAND
Printed in Great Britain by Butler & Tanner Ltd., Frome and London

CONTENTS AND COLOUR PLATES

CONTENTS AND COLOUR PLATES

CONTENTS AND COLOUR PLATES

PREFACE

THE first glimpse we get of the author of these Fables shows him to us very clearly, although we have to look back twenty-five centuries. A party is setting out for Ephesus, and one of the slaves, an odd-looking fellow who, because of his dark skin, has been nicknamed Æsop, or Ethiopian, shrewdly takes as his share of the load the bread to be eaten on the journey, which, of course, will be diminishing all the time. Later, we see Æsop, now a freed man, employed on important missions by the rich King Crœsus.

The stories in this book are not direct translations from any of the numerous Greek and Latin editions of *Æsop's Fables*, but have been rewritten for modern children. Some of the longer stories, for example "The Little Partridge's Stolen Eggs" (a perfect gem), are taken directly from the old Indian tales of the *Hitopadesa*, a source from which Æsop himself drew freely. There has been no alteration of Æsop's natural history, which is wonderfully correct, according to the knowledge of his time. Frogs *can* distend themselves with air; the lonely bat is *not* a bird, although it looks like one; and men at times are as absurd as the bewildered astronomer who found a dragon in the moon, or the priceless noodles who fought for the donkey's shadow.

" The traveller and the Arab made such a noise with their shouts and blows that the donkey took fright and galloped away. So there they were left, not only without the shadow, but without the donkey."

ÆSOP'S FABLES

THE DONKEY AND HIS SHADOW

ONE fine morning, in a sunny Eastern country, an Arab stood with his donkey at the door of an inn. The donkey was for hire; and the Arab knew there were travellers sleeping at the inn who would be glad to engage such a fine animal to carry them across the desert. Sure enough, as the Arab waited, one of the travellers came out. Seeing the donkey, he asked if he could hire it. The Arab said " Yes," and the two agreed upon the sum that the traveller should pay for the donkey to carry him over the hot sands to the city on the other side.

They set off at once, the traveller and all his baggage on the donkey, the Arab walking behind. The Arab was used to the desert, and did not much mind the long tramp. He munched a green lettuce nearly as big as his head, and thought cheerfully of the money the traveller was to pay him at the end of the journey.

THE DONKEY AND HIS SHADOW

They moved on steadily for a time, the three of them—traveller, donkey and Arab. But, as the day wore on, the sun grew very hot, and they all got very tired. The traveller decided that he would like to rest for an hour or two, so he pulled up the donkey, got off its back, and, seeing that it threw a nice, big, cool shadow on the sand, sat down to rest in this convenient bit of shade.

There was no room for the Arab in the donkey's shadow, so he had to sit in the hot sunshine outside. For a little time he stared gloomily and resentfully at the traveller, while the perspiration trickled from his forehead. Suddenly an idea struck him. Springing to his feet, he caught the donkey by the bridle, led him a few steps forward, and, when a nice new shadow fell from the donkey on to the sand, plumped himself down in the middle of it.

The traveller had been asleep, but he awoke with a start of rage. Up he jumped, and strode off after the donkey and the shadow. But when he tried to sit down, the Arab drove him off.

" No ! No ! " said he. " The donkey is mine ! Therefore the shadow is mine ! Go away ! "

" The shadow yours, indeed ! " replied the traveller furiously. " How dare you say so. *I* hired the donkey ! Therefore I hired the shadow as well ! "

THE DONKEY AND HIS SHADOW

"That is not so!" insisted the Arab. "If you wanted to hire the shadow, you should have said so at the beginning. I should then have charged you more for it!"

The traveller, instead of answering, seized the donkey by the bridle, and walked a few paces with it, shadow and all. Then down he sat, once more in the donkey's shade. But the Arab, springing after him, did not argue the matter this time. Instead, he lost his temper entirely, and gave the traveller a cuff on the head.

The traveller replied with another cuff, and, in a few seconds, the two were engaged in a furious battle! They made such a noise with their shouts and blows that the donkey took fright. Giving a loud bray of dismay, he flung up his heels, stuck down his head, bucked off the traveller's bundles, and galloped away, at full speed, back to the inn, taking his shadow with him!

So there they were left, the silly traveller and the still sillier Arab, not only without the shadow, but without the donkey. There was nothing for them to do but to pick up the bundles, take their staffs in their hands, and follow the donkey, a lesson to everybody that folk may easily lose the substance if they spend their time in fighting over the shadow.

CRYING " WOLF "

ONCE upon a time the hills and woods were as full of wolves as now they are full of foxes ; and in some places, a good deal fuller. In the summer-time the wolves stayed among the trees and caves and brought up their families. But in the winter, when the snow was on the ground, and most of the other wild things had buried themselves and gone to sleep for the season, the wolves used to get very hungry—so hungry that they took to stealing from the hill sheep-folds.

The great beasts did not go thieving singly, but banded themselves in packs. If a shepherd, sitting inside his little stone hut of an evening, heard a scuffling among his poor sheep, and saw a long, lean grey shadow sneaking near the flock, he knew very well that half a dozen more such shadows would soon come creeping from the edge of the forest into the open. Then woe betide the helpless woolly sheep !

So all the shepherds in the district agreed to help each other. If anyone among them saw a

"'Wolf! Wolf! Wolf!' he shrieked at the top of his voice."

B*

wolf, he was immediately to jump on to a rock or a high mound, and shout "Wolf! Wolf!" with all his might. Then his friends and neighbours would instantly seize their sticks and clubs, and, rushing to the spot, help to drive away the thief and his companions.

Well, this plan answered extremely well, and now the shepherds hardly ever lost any of their sheep. They had only to shout "Wolf! Wolf! Wolf!" at any hour of the night, and all the other shepherds came running one after another along the mountain paths and through the deep gullies of rock and furze bushes. As fast as the shepherds ran into the sheep-fold the wolves ran out! They were frightened of such a lot of strong men with even stronger sticks.

Then, one day, one of the older shepherds had to go to the town for a few days, and leave his son in charge of the sheep. This son was as foolish a fellow as you could wish to see marry a clever wife. He was a dreadful coward, too, and horribly frightened at the thought of the wolves that came into the folds after the sheep. So he prepared to sit up all night by his fire of faggots, nursing a great club.

The sun set, and the moon rose, and the unhappy shepherd-boy sat nervously clutching his club. All at once he was quite sure he heard a growl, and saw a long lean shape slip out from among the pines. He sprang to his feet in great excitement.

" Wolf ! Wolf ! Wolf ! " he shrieked at the top of his voice, brandishing his club wildly. And over the hilltop, and up through the gullies, ran the shepherds, quite ready for the fight.

They found the silly youth racing up and down among the sheep, which were frightened to death. But it was their own shepherd who was scaring them, for there was not a wolf within miles.

Warning the foolish boy not to call them from their warm beds for nothing, the shepherds returned home. But they had no sooner settled down in their own huts again than a still more frenzied call of " Wolf ! Wolf ! Wolf ! " brought them all out a second time. And, a second time, they discovered that there was no wolf at all—nothing but a frightened lad clubbing shadows thrown by the moon.

They scolded him severely, and told him that, if he wanted to club shadows, he could club them by himself ; and that, if he really saw a wolf, he would know very well what it was like. Then they walked off by twos and threes, extremely cold and sleepy and cross.

This time they had not even reached their homes before " Wolf ! Wolf ! Wolf ! " sounded after them, in a perfect shriek of terror. But the shepherds shook their wise grey heads and grunted into their wise grey beards.

"Not so!" said they to each other. "We know better by this time. It's just moon-shadows again!" And they all went home to bed.

But it really *had* been a wolf at last! And, following the wolf, came all the pack, running and leaping and jostling among the sheep. They ate up as many as they wanted, and, last of all, they ate the foolish shepherd-boy himself. So his father, when he came home, put up a little tombstone to his memory among the hills, and there, to the best of my belief, it stands to this day.

What do you think is written on it?

Well, it does not take much guessing. I am quite sure all of you have often heard the silly shepherd's epitaph.

"If folks cry 'Wolf' for shadows, nobody will hurry to their rescue when a real wolf comes along with teeth and claws."

THE STORY OF THE BAT

ONE fine morning the sun, as it climbed over the eastern shoulder of the hill, looked down upon a strange sight. In the middle of the plain below were drawn up two armies. One army was a mass of big horned heads, and little woolly heads, and long tails, and short tails, and bodies either rough and furry or hairy and smooth. These were the regiments of the beasts, and they were quite ready for battle.

Opposite them stood the enemy army. Here you might see what looked like an ocean of colour, trembling with a thousand wings. All about these lovely wings the sunbeams flashed as they might flash about a lot of jewels. It was the army of the birds, and they were as pretty as a field of flowers in May.

Their commander, who must certainly have been an eagle, stood waiting for the beasts to charge; and we can hardly doubt that the beasts were led by their King, the lion himself. But the beasts paused for a moment. Their chiefs had gathered about a curious, small, winged creature, just arrived in their midst.

" Who are you ? " they asked the new-comer doubtfully. " We do not think you are a beast, for you have wings ! "

The little animal looked at the fine army which stood round about him, and answered with determination.

" People call me a bat," said he. " But I am most certainly a beast. I have fur all over me, and four legs, and a lot of teeth. Look at them ! "

He opened his mouth widely and the chiefs of the army peered inside. Sure enough, there were the teeth !

" You want to join our army, then, and to fight with us ? " said the beasts.

They could not deny his fur, and his four legs, and his teeth, though they thought him the oddest little beast in the world. His middle finger was as long as his head and body put together, and he had a hook instead of a thumb.

" To be sure I do ! " said the bat. " I would not fight on the side of those silly birds for anything."

So the beasts let him join their army, and the fight began.

But the bat—who was a terrible little coward —did nothing but flit about above the regi-ments and look on. From this safe position he perceived, by and by, that the beasts were getting the worst of it.

Off flew Mr. Bat, sneaking through a dark wood that grew near at hand. Flitting silently out from the shelter of the trees he arrived, breathless, in the middle of the birds.

" Who are you ? " cried the chief of the birds. " And what do you want here ? "

" People call me a bat ! " answered the little coward. " But I am most certainly a bird. Don't you see that I can fly ? I have flown here, with all my might, to tell you what our awful enemies, the terrible beasts, are doing over yonder ! "

He told the birds everything that they wanted to know about the plans of the beasts, and assured his new friends that the other army was on the verge of being beaten. So the birds rushed joyfully into the fight again, while the cowardly bat flitted about in the safest places, as before.

But, by and by, the tide of battle turned. And now the birds had to fall back for a time, defeated. What did Mr. Bat do but take wing as fast as possible, and set off through the wood a second time, to rejoin the beasts ?

But his cowardice was found out. Some birds had been posted in the wood as sentries, and when they saw Mr. Bat flitting cautiously through the trees, they flew after him, and took him prisoner !

" Who are you ? " they demanded, fiercely. " And where are you going ? "

The bat began to shake with fright. He didn't know how to answer. If he said he was a beast, the sentries would probably kill him ; if he said he was a bird they would tell him he must be a spy going off to give information to the enemy. So he stammered, and stuttered, and made excuses, until the sentries, out of patience, flew back with him to the bird army, and took him to their chiefs.

There was great joy, at that minute, among the regiments of the birds. The battle had turned in their favour just after Mr. Bat had flown off, and now they were congratulating each other excitedly on a complete victory. You can imagine the noise of all those birds talking at once.

" Why, here is that funny little thing again, brought back as a prisoner ! " said they. " What has he been doing, and is he really a bird or a beast ? "

" Oh, I'm a bird—I'm a bird ! " cried the wretched little bat. " I was flying through the wood to get secret information for you when your sentries took me prisoner. But if I had told them this they would not have believed me !

THE STORY OF THE BAT

You, my lords, can trust me! Remember what valuable news I brought you before! Surely that should convince you which side I have been upon all through!"

Unfortunately for the bat, the birds, at that moment, began to bring in other prisoners of war. Among the prisoners were many beasts who remembered the bat, and who, not knowing what had happened, hailed him as one of themselves. So then the chiefs of the birds held a court-martial, and the bat was tried for his life. The court-martial did not execute him, however, but punished him in a very suitable manner.

" Because you have said first that you were a bird and then that you were a beast," declared the head of the court-martial, solemnly, " you are condemned to be neither! You shall live all by yourself, shall only fly by night, and shall spend the hours of daylight hanging in dark, out-of-the-way places, by means of your ridiculous thumb, which is nothing but a hook! As for your knees, they shall always be turned inside out, so that you will never be able to walk properly! And anybody who catches you, and sees the odd little thing you are, will declare that you are quite alone in the order of creation, and belong neither to the birds nor to the beasts!"

And that this story is true you can find out

" The sentries, out of patience, flew back with the bat to the bird army."

for yourselves if, some fine day, you manage to catch a bat in a barn or a cave, and look at his funny wings, and his furry body, and his tiny teeth, and his thumb that, thousands and thousands of years ago, turned into a hook!

THE FROG AND THE OX

ONE day a lot of little frogs, just grown up from tadpoles, were jumping and playing among the flowers that grew on the edge of a pond. In the meadow beyond a herd of cattle were feeding; and by and by a big young ox left the others and came tramp, tramp, tramp, down to the pool to drink. His great horny feet, going squish-squash through the soft mud, plumped right into the middle of the family of frogs, and crushed all but one of them to death.

This one went scrambling and hopping away among the reeds to find his mother, who was sitting on a water-lily leaf, croaking a tune to herself. When she saw the little frog she asked what had happened. Breathless and terrified, he told his story.

" Oh, mother, a beast—such a dreadful beast —has killed all my brothers and sisters ! He had a foot as large as twenty frogs put together, and he put it, plump, on to the tops of their heads ! "

31

" With that the mother frog set to work to blow herself out with air. Then, holding her breath carefully, she demanded :
'Was your strange monster as big as *that* ? ' "

THE FROG AND THE OX

" A beast with a foot as big as twenty frogs put together ! " exclaimed the mother, turning from green to yellow with rage. " Such an animal cannot be allowed to come into our meadow. I will go and fight him ! "

" Oh, mother ! " croaked the little frog hoarsely, " you cannot fight him ! He is much too big ! "

" Rubbish ! " said the mother. " However big he is I can make myself bigger ! "

With that she set to work to blow herself out with air. For as frogs have no ribs, they can swallow air much as children can swallow milk ! And she swallowed mouthful after mouthful until she was swollen to twice her natural size. Then, holding her breath carefully, she demanded :

" Was your strange monster as big as *that* ? "

" Oh, mother," cried the little frog in a fright, " he was ever so much bigger—nearly as big as a mountain. And pray stop swelling yourself out with air, or you will certainly burst ! "

" Rubbish," said the mother again. " You don't know how much air I can swallow ! If the strange beast was as big as a mountain I will go on swelling until I am as big as a mountain, too."

And, with that, she shut her eyes and, opening her mouth as wide as it would stretch, swallowed more and more air, while the little frog looked on in a terrible fright. But, at last, as she had no ribs, she *did* burst; and the sound of the bursting made quite an explosion in Frog-land, so that all the other frogs came running to see what was the matter. The little frog, weeping over the remains, explained that his mother had burst in trying to make herself big enough to go and fight the ox who had squashed all his brothers and sisters.

"Foolish creature!" said a very old frog, gravely wagging his head. "Of what use was it to puff herself out in that way? Even if she had made herself as big as her enemy, she would only have had air inside, after all. And, as it was, she did not manage to do anything but burst!"

THE MAN WHO STARED AT THE STARS

THERE was once a man who was always staring at the stars, wondering what they were, and how they hung in the sky.

If he had been a sensible sort of man he would have bought a telescope, and built himself a tower on top of the roof. But, instead, he used to wander out at night in the inky darkness, staring up at the sky, and taking no heed of where he was going.

The result was that, one dark evening, when the earth was full of shadows as the heavens were full of stars, this dreamy man fell head-over-heels into a well. Luckily for him, the well was dry, so he sat up on a heap of leaves at the bottom, and shouted loudly for help. Presently in the dim light he saw a head peering over the top of the well, and recognized a neighbour's voice, saying:

"Who in the world is down there at the bottom of my old dry well?"

"It is I!" called the unfortunate star-gazer. "For pity's sake bring a rope and pull me out!"

" The result was that, one dark evening, when the earth was full of shadows as the heavens were full of stars, the dreamy man fell head-over-heels into a well."

C*

" *You!* " cried the other, preparing to fetch the rope. " Then, now that you are at the bottom of the well, I'll give you a piece of sound advice. Don't be so keen on studying things that are hung over your head in the sky until you have discovered those that lie at your feet on the earth! "

THE LITTLE CRAB AND THE BIG CRAB

A LITTLE crab was crawling with its funny hard-jointed legs across the rocks of the sea shore, on its way to a cool and delightful pool full of pink and green sea-anemones. It went this way, and that way, and the other way—not because it wanted to, but because it couldn't help it. A big crab, seated in the shadow of a weedy stone, was watching it with a pair of queer bulgy eyes set somewhere about its middle.

" Oh, my dear little friend," said the big crab condescendingly, " Where are you trying to get ? Are you going north, south, east or west ? "

" I am going to the anemone-pool over there," said the little crab breathlessly. And it waved a tired claw vaguely over its shoulder.

" Then walk straight ! Walk straight ! " exclaimed the big crab. " You will never get anywhere at all if you walk so crookedly."

The little crab sat down among the limpets and sighed.

" Pray show me how to do so ! " it said. And

THE LITTLE CRAB AND THE BIG CRAB

it folded its legs as meekly beneath its body as a good little school-girl might fold her hands on her lap.

Out came the big crab from the sea-weed, and set off towards the anemone-pool. But, like the little crab, it might, for all one knew, have been going north, south, east or west. It could no more walk straight than the little crab it had been lecturing so wisely.

" Oh, dear ! Oh, dear ! " sighed the little crab. " It is quite plain I shall have to go on walking crookedly, since not even the biggest crab in our family can show me the way to walk straight ! "

THE LION AND THE MOUSE

A GREAT lion, well contented after an excellent supper, had fallen asleep at the door of his cave. He was dreaming of all sorts of nice things—mostly things to eat —when he felt a little tug at his mane. Drowsily lifting a paw, he caught a mouse!

"*G-r-r-r-r-r!*" growled the lion. "What is a miserable thing like you doing in my mane? You woke me from a most delightful dream. I shall eat you up!"

"Oh, your Majesty! your Majesty!" squeaked the mouse, "please spare me! I had no idea you were a lion. I thought you were a haystack! And I wanted some nice hay to line my new nest with. But, if you will forgive me and let me go, I will repay you some day. One good turn deserves another!"

The lion burst out laughing. He was so amused by the mouse's argument that he felt he could not eat such a funny little creature up. So he let Mr. Mouse go, and went to sleep again, chuckling to himself and murmuring: "'One good

turn deserves another!' What a deliciously conceited little mouse!"

In the cool dawn Mr. Lion woke, stretched
himself, decided that it was going to be a fine
day, and went hunting in the forest. But, instead
of being the hunter, he soon became the hunted.
A party from the King's palace, hard by, were
looking for lions that morning—not to kill, but
to put in dens in the Royal Zoological Gardens.
All great kings kept lions in those days; the more
lions they had in their gardens the more highly
they were thought of by their neighbours.

Soon the hunters caught sight of the great
tracks made by Mr. Lion through the tall tangled
grass. After him they went, and presently caught
him and tied him up with strong ropes. Then
they left the lion prostrate on the ground, while
they hurried off for the cage in which he was to
be taken to the King's Gardens.

" *G-r-r-r-r* !" roared the lion. " *H-r-r-r-
umph* !"

He tugged at the ropes in vain; but, a short
distance off, a tiny mouse sat up and pricked its
ears.

" *G-r-r-r-r-r* ! *H-r-r-r-umph* !" roared the lion
again.

" I know that voice," murmured the mouse.
Off it pattered, at full speed, in the direction
of the roars. There it found Mr. Lion, tugging

45

at the ropes, and making as much noise as a thunderstorm.

" Pray keep still ! " squeaked the mouse. " I have a better way with ropes than you have. Don't move, and I will set you free ! "

The little mouse set his tiny white teeth to the ropes, and began to gnaw. And he gnawed first through one rope, and then through another, till, just as the sound of the hunters coming with the cage echoed through the forest, the lion stood up, quite free.

" I told you I would repay you some day ! " cried the mouse triumphantly. " Now, you see, I have kept my word. Even a tiny mouse can help a lion."

And he twiddled his whiskers, waved his tail, and scampered away into the bushes.

THE GROANING MOUNTAIN

LONG ago, in a far country, a big mountain lifted its purple head high over the village in the valley. It was a very magnificent mountain indeed, with pine-trees on the slopes, and great precipices beneath it. For hundreds of years it had sent its long shadow down the valley in silence, and no sounds had been heard from it but those made by the screaming hawks, and the waterfalls, and the wild winds that sometimes blew through the trees.

Then, one day, a most remarkable thing happened. The people in the village distinctly heard the mountain groan!

It was such an amazing sound that everybody stopped what they were doing and stood still to listen. The maids and men ceased milking, the hay-makers dropped their scythes, and the farmers' wives let their bread burn in the ovens as they ran out into the orchards to see what was the matter. However the sky and the fields and the distant sea looked the same as usual; and by and by folks began to enquire from each other if they had not been mistaken. But even while they were asking the question, the mountain gave a second groan, much louder than the first.

It really was a dreadful noise, and this time the people who lived quite a long way off heard it too. Presently they began to arrive at the village in little groups, asking everybody they met what had happened. Nobody knew anything except that the mountain had groaned, as if it were in dreadful pain and trouble. Some of the men thought it was the beginning of an earthquake ; but the women said they believed the mountain was groaning because a giant that was inside it was trying to get out.

They discussed the question anxiously, standing in crowds round the foot of the mountain. Those who believed in the giant pointed to the great cracks in the slopes, and said that surely these must have been made by giants breaking out of some hidden caves. Gradually the men who at first had believed in the earthquake grew to believe in the giant. Meanwhile the mountain groaned louder and louder, and more and more frequently, and other people arrived from villages that were miles and miles away, and joined in the discussions about the earthquake and the giant.

At last the mountain—which was now giving

" So everybody went home, laughing at the
mountain that had made such a dreadful
to-do all the morning, and then had nothing
to show for the fuss but one teeny-weeny
mouse ! "

about thirty awful groans a minute—let out a perfect yell! At the same moment a really enormous crack showed in its side. The people held their breath, and some of them covered their eyes in terror. Dead silence followed, and then—what do you think happened?

Down the path that led to the village from the enormous crack in the mountain slope, its tiny feet making no sound on the stones, its long tail waving, and its bright eyes glancing timidly from side to side, scampered a mouse! When it saw the crowds it gave a little squeak of terror, and ran away into the long grass!

The people still waited, but now the mountain was quite quiet again! Not a single groan came out of the sides or the top. So everybody went home, laughing at the mountain that had made such a dreadful to-do all the morning, and then had nothing to show for the fuss but one teeny-weeny mouse!

THE RAVEN AND THE SWAN

DOWN among the brown-headed bulrushes, the purple loose-strife, the yellow iris, and the pale lilies of a quiet river, floated a snow-white swan. He was beautiful to look at, with his long curved neck, his proud head, and his bright eyes. His wife sat on a little mound of sticks, which he had helped her to make, in a quiet backwater surrounded by green reeds. Under her breast were six big eggs. She watched her husband admiringly from her nest, as he swam up and down, guarding her. If anybody went too near her, he arched his lovely wings till they almost met over his head, and hissed with anger.

Hopping about on the bank, not far away, was an ugly black raven. He was short of food at the moment, and had come some way to find it. Almost any kind of bone made a dinner for the raven; and he generally lived among the mountains, where all sorts of poor little dead creatures could be found. Nobody liked the raven, partly because of what he ate. The boys

53

would throw stones at him, and the girls would say, "Ugh! Isn't he ugly and nasty?" But both boys and girls called to each other with delight when they saw the beautiful snow-white swan.

Well, the raven felt very annoyed about this. He hid himself in a clump of reeds, and peeped through the stalks at the swan, who found his food by dipping his long shining neck deep into the water. The raven noticed that he hardly ever came out of the stream, unless he took a seat on the nest for a little time, to relieve his wife. And the ugly black bird made up his mind that the swan was white because he was washed by the water of the river, not only all day, but all night as well.

"That being the case," croaked the raven to himself, "*I* will live in the stream, as the swan lives, and very soon *I* shall be white and beautiful, too."

So the silly bird came out from behind the reeds and hopped, as far as he dared, into the shallow part of the river. He was afraid to hop too far, because he could not swim, and he did not wish to be drowned. But, in every other way, he did just as the swan did. He dabbled always on the edge of the water; he arched his wings over his head, as well as he could; and he stuck his dark head and neck deep into the

" The raven did just as the swan did. He dabbled
always on the edge of the water ; he arched
his wings over his head, as well as he could ;
and he stuck his dark head and neck deep
into the pools where the pale water-buttercups grew."

pools where the pale water-buttercups grew. But, beyond nearly choking himself with weeds, he found that nothing happened ; for how should he know that the swan, when *he* did it, was merely catching and eating the frogs' eggs which made such delicious water-jellies ?

This went on for quite a long time. The swan continued to lead his stately life, day by day, hardly noticing that the raven was there, imitating him. Now and then his proud, calm eyes would catch sight of a strange black bird, fussing about among the lilies—but that was all. The raven, meanwhile, grew uglier and uglier, and thinner and thinner. But he was of an obstinate nature, and would not give in, nor go back to the mountains, where the food on which he lived could always be found.

At last, after having had nothing to eat for many days, the raven died. His body, with the claws sticking straight up, was seen by the swan among the reeds. The swan wondered what it was, and then floated away again, dipping his head and neck deep into the water to catch more jellies. He had no idea that the ugly dead thing was a raven, who had been copying him for days in order to become white and beautiful ; but who had remained as black as ever, and, in the end, had merely died of starvation.

THE TREASURE IN THE ORCHARD

AN old gardener who was dying sent for his two sons to come to his bedside, as he wished to speak to them. They came in answer to his request, and, raising himself on his pillows, the old man pointed through the window towards his orchard.

" You see the orchard ? " said he, feebly.

" Yes, Father, we see the orchard."

" For years it has given the best of fruit— golden oranges, amber apricots, and cherries bigger and brighter than rubies ! "

" To be sure, Father. It has always been a good orchard ! "

The old gardener nodded his head, time and time again. He looked at his hands—they were worn with the spade that he had used all his life. Then he looked at the hands of his sons, and saw that the nails were polished and the fingers white as those of any fine lady's.

" You have never done a day's work in your lives, you two ! " said he. " I doubt if you ever will ! But I have hidden a treasure in my

"The two sons dug and they dug, day after day, and week after week."

orchard for you to find. You will never possess
it unless you dig it up. It lies mid-way between
two of the trees, not too near, yet not too far
from the trunks. It is yours for the trouble of
digging—that is all !

Then he sent them away, and soon afterwards
he died. So the orchard became the property
of his sons, and, without any delay, they set
to work to dig for the treasure that had been
promised them.

Well, they dug and they dug, day after day, and
week after week, going down the long alleys of
fruit trees, never too near yet never too far from
the trunks. They dug up all the weeds, and
picked out all the stones ; not because they liked
weeding and cleaning, but because it was all
part of the hunt for the buried treasure. Winter
passed and spring came, and never were there
such blossoms as those which hung the orange
and apricots and cherry trees with curtains of
petals pale as pearls and soft as silk. Then
summer threw sunshine over the orchard, and
sometimes the clouds bathed it in cool, delicious
rain. At last the time of the fruit harvest came.
But the two brothers had not yet found the
treasure that was hidden among the roots of the
trees.

Then they sent for a merchant from the nearest
town to buy the fruit. It hung in great bunches,

golden oranges, amber apricots, and cherries bigger and brighter than rubies. The merchant looked at them in open admiration.

"This is the finest crop I have yet seen," said he. "I will give you twenty bags of money for it!"

Twenty bags of money was more than the two brothers had ever owned in their life. They struck the bargain in great delight, and took the money-bags into the house, while the merchant made arrangements to carry away the fruit.

"I will come again next year," said he. "I am always glad to buy a crop like this. *How you must have dug and weeded and worked to get it!*"

He went away, and the brothers sat eyeing each other over the tops of the money-bags. Their hands were rough and toil-worn, just as the old gardener's had been when he died.

"Golden oranges and amber apples and cherries bigger and brighter than rubies," said one of them, softly. "I believe that that is the treasure we have been digging for all the year, the very treasure that our father meant!"

THE MILLER'S DONKEY

ONE day a miller, who owned a very strong donkey, decided to sell it; so he and his little boy set off to the town together, driving the animal in front of them. As they went, they came across a party of girls, merry-making between the flowering hawthorn hedges, as girls will always merry-make on a fine morning in May. When they saw the old man and the little boy trudging sedately behind the lusty donkey they began to laugh.

"See those two silly fellows!" said they to each other. "They've got a fine donkey, and, instead of prancing on his back, they crawl at his heels! Who ever saw such an absurd thing? Why, if they had a coach and four they'd likely only run at the wheels, instead of sitting on the cushions inside!"

The old miller, when he heard this, was very vexed. Instantly he made his son mount the donkey and sit comfortably astride its broad back. For his part, however, he continued to walk behind.

THE MILLER'S DONKEY

By and by they met another party, not of young girls, but of old men. They were wagging their grey heads solemnly, and talking, as old men will, of the bad manners of the young.

"There!" exclaimed one, the moment he caught sight of the miller's son on the donkey. "Is not that proof of what we have just been saying? No respect is shown to the old nowadays! Look at that strong young lad riding at his ease, while his poor old father kicks up the dust with his toes! Get down, youngster, that your tired parent may get up!"

The miller was quite upset by this new criticism, and hastily made his son dismount. Then he, himself, got on to the donkey's back, while his little boy walked alongside. The child's legs were shorter than the donkey's, and he had hard work to keep up. So that some women who were spreading their washing on the hedges began to scold the miller shrilly.

"If that was *my* child," cried one of them, "he wouldn't be tiring himself to death trotting at your stirrup, you selfish old man! You to call yourself a father! You're not worthy to have a son at all!"

"Oh, dear! Oh, dear!" sighed the poor miller. "It seems that I've done wrong again! Get up, sonny, and ride behind! We'll see if anybody abuses us then!"

THE MILLER'S DONKEY

So the son got up and rode behind. But in a short time they met a farmer, who looked them over most indignantly.

" Pray, sir," said he to the miller, " Is that poor unhappy little donkey your own ? "

" Certainly it is my own," replied the miller. " Why do you ask ? "

" Because I couldn't have believed it ! " answered the farmer. " Nobody but a fool would overload his beast like that ! You and that lad there are much better able to carry the donkey than the donkey is to carry you ! Why don't the pair of you get down and try it ? "

He was poking fun, you see, and did not really mean what he said. But the foolish miller once more took it for granted that the last speaker spoke the soundest sense. Down he got—he and his son as well. Then, with a good deal of difficulty, they tied the poor donkey's legs together, and slung it on a long pole, which they bought from a waggoner on the roadside.

" Now," panted the miller, out of breath, but always in earnest, " take one end of the pole, my lad, and I will take the other. Then we will carry the donkey across the bridge yonder, and so into the town which lies just on the other side of the water."

By this time a crowd had collected, which really was not surprising. They stood and roared with laughter as the miller and his little boy tried to shoulder the pole, with the donkey, braying loudly, hanging upside down. But the effort was too much for the pair of them. Down went pole and donkey with a crash, and away they rolled into the river, where they disappeared under water, and never came up again !

Then, at last the miller, wringing his hands, began to declare that he had made a fool of himself. Taking it all round, it was a pity that he did not make the discovery a little earlier !

" I have tried to please everybody ! " he lamented loudly, " and I have satisfied no one —least of all myself ! This is the result of taking one piece of advice after another ! Next time I want to do a thing I will do it my own way."

THE DONKEY AND THE LAP-DOG

A MAN once owned a donkey and a beautiful little Maltese dog. The donkey lived in a nice warm stable, and was fed every night and morning with hay and oats, and given a good long drink of water out of a pail. He was a big, strong donkey, and his master had plenty of work for him to do. Some days he had to walk round and round in a circle, turning the wheel that helped to grind the corn ; sometimes he was taken into the quiet forest and driven home laden with wood for the fire ; and sometimes he had great flour-sacks bound on to his back to carry into the town for sale.

While the donkey did these useful things, the tiny Maltese dog did nothing at all but play and frisk about. Now and then it jumped on to its master's lap, and, setting its paws on his shoulders, tried to lick his face. Then the man would laugh, and fondle it, and give it nice bits of cake to eat and milk to drink. The more the tiny dog capered and pranced, the more its master petted it. So that the donkey, who could see what was going on through the window grew very jealous of the Maltese, and began to compare his own lot with that of the spoilt little dog.

"That ridiculous creature!" he grumbled one evening as he crunched his oats. "It does nothing but play antics! I suppose it is on account of such absurdities that the man is so fond of it! Well, well! There is nothing easier in the world than gambolling! I did it, myself, when I was a foal. I have a good mind to imitate the ways of the Maltese! Then my master will think the world of me, and I shall live a gloriously idle life, and have the best of everything to eat."

He thought over the plan all night, and in the morning, when he was let out of his stable, instead of waiting quietly for his halter to be put on, as usual, he suddenly galloped off! Across the yard he went, helter-skelter, jumped the hedge, and took the garden in three bucks, like a rabbit! The man was sitting at breakfast, inside the house. You can guess his amazement when suddenly the donkey appeared at the door of the room, rushed round the table, and, putting his great fore-feet into his master's lap, opened an enormous hairy mouth, stuck out a big pink tongue and tried to lick the man's face!

Up jumped the man, with a shout of anger,

" The donkey, putting his great fore-feet into his master's lap, opened an enormous hairy mouth, stuck out a big pink tongue and tried to lick the man's face."

but the donkey only gave a playful leap. He did his best to bark merrily, like the Maltese (who, in an awful fright, had jumped out of the window, as well he might) but he only succeeded in producing a hideous bray. Down crashed the milk-jug, the porridge-bowl, the honey, and the nice new bread. The man rushed off for a big stick; but the donkey, thinking he was making a great impression, only went on waltzing round the table.

He quickly learnt his mistake. Back came his master with the stick, and a halter, and half a dozen servants, and an end was soon put to foolish Mr. Donkey's dance. He was hurried back to his stable, and given the soundest beating he had ever had in his life. Then he was marched off to the mill, and set to work the whole day in grinding the corn.

" Oh, dear ! Oh, dear," he said to himself, as, sore and dejected, he walked round and round, "it is evident that I have been a very silly donkey indeed ! I was not meant to dance and play round the breakfast table, nor to sit in my master's lap ! In future I will do everything that is wise and useful, and will be content with my nice warm stable, my sound oats, and my sweet dry hay ! "

THE GOOSE WHO LAID GOLDEN EGGS

ONCE upon a time a poor peasant was seated at the door of his hut, wondering where he should get food in the coming winter. He had no money to buy it with, and he was growing too old to work. As he sat there, a stranger appeared before him, carrying a beautiful white goose.

" Take care of my goose," said the stranger, " and my goose will take care of you ! "

He set the goose down on the ground, and vanished as suddenly as he had appeared. Then the peasant knew that he was a fairy in disguise, and that the goose was an enchanted goose. So he took the great white bird into his cottage and gave her water to drink and his last handful of oatmeal to eat. When the goose had finished her supper, the peasant made her a nest to sleep in, out of warm sweet hay.

He went to bed, himself, and slept soundly. In the morning he was wakened by a triumphant cackling from the goose. Going to the nest, he looked inside. And what do you think he saw

" And what do you think he saw there ?   Nothing more nor less than a beautiful golden egg ! "

there ? Nothing more nor less than a beautiful golden egg !

How surprised and overjoyed the peasant was, to be sure. He picked up the egg and held it to the light, while the clever goose went on cackling proudly, as if she knew what a wonderful thing she had done.

The peasant hurried off to the nearest town, and sold his golden egg for a great many pieces of money. Then he bought oats and wheat for the goose, and white bread and wine and honey for himself. Hastening back, he lit a fire in his cottage, and sat down to an excellent breakfast, together with the goose.

The next morning the same thing happened, and the next, and the next. The peasant was soon able to buy new chairs, and a table, and warm clothes. Then he grew rich enough to purchase a bigger house, and to plant a garden round about it with trees and flowers. He made a special corner for the goose, who strolled contentedly about under the rose-trees on the lawn, and laid a golden egg to shine in her nest as regularly as the sun rose to shine in the sky.

But, sad to tell, his riches began to turn the peasant's head. He grew hard and greedy, and wanted more and more eggs. He began to wonder how many more the goose had inside her, and to think he would like to have all the eggs at once, instead of only getting seven a week. So the unkind, cruel fellow, one sad day, killed the goose that laid the golden eggs!

And, when he opened her white body, there was not a single egg to be seen!

He stared, with horror-stricken eyes, at the poor dead goose, and then he started to do his best to bring her to life again. But it was no good. While he was trying, all at once the stranger appeared again at his side.

"I told you to take care of my goose, and my goose would take care of you!" he said reproachfully.

Then he picked up the dead goose and carried her away, and, as he was a fairy, no doubt he knew how to bring her to life again. But the greedy, cruel peasant began to grow poor as quickly as he had grown rich, for never again was he able to go to the goose's nest and gather up her beautiful golden eggs

THE ENCHANTED CAT

IN a beautiful castle that must have been built on the very edge of Fairyland—if not quite inside the borders—lived a brave and handsome Prince. He did all the things that other princes did; hunted, swam, played games with balls and heavy weights, and went shooting in the woods with a magnificent bow and arrows. All the princesses for leagues round his home wanted to marry him. But who do you think was more deeply in love with him than anyone else? Why, none other than the castle cat!

She was a pretty cat, and the Prince was quite fond of her. He would rub her head when she came purring round his ankles, and say to her jokingly, "Why, Puss, you have green eyes, just like a nymph who lives under a fountain!" Then the cat would give a little mew. The mew meant all sorts of things that, of course, the Prince could not understand.

At last the cat's love for the Prince became so intense that the poor little creature could

" But who do you think was more deeply in love
with the Prince than anyone else ? Why,
none other than the castle cat ! "

neither eat nor sleep, and even forgot to lick her paws and wash her ears. She just sat on the rug and moped. The Prince, when he saw her, would say, " Puss, you are getting terribly thin ! " But he had no idea that she was getting thin with hopeless admiration for himself.

Then, one day, a certain fairy lady who was well known in those times, and who was called the Queen of Love, happened to come driving over the castle roofs in a chariot of mother-o'-pearl, drawn by a team of beautiful white doves. She heard the long, sorrowful sighing of somebody who was dying for love, and recognized the sound instantly. Pulling up her doves, she peeped down the chimney and saw the cat !

" What is it you want ? " asked this exquisite lady. " I heard the sighs that only true lovers give ! Who, then, is it that you care for so deeply ? "

The cat, not at all startled, peeped back up the chimney at the lady and the doves.

" Dear Queen ! " she answered (for she knew who it was immediately), " I am in love with the Prince of this palace ! I simply adore him. But I have no hope. Though to me he is the most magnificent Prince in creation, to him I am only the castle cat ! "

" Do you love him so much that you could

change your whole nature for him?" asked the
lady at the top of the chimney.

"Try me and see!" answered the cat. "If
you will only turn me into a beautiful maiden I
will never, never, never give the least sign that
I was once a cat!"

"H'm!" said the lovely lady doubtfully.
But she waved her wand down the chimney,
before she flew off with her doves.

The cat gave a sort of little mew—but the
sound ended in something like "ince!" She
opened her mouth again, and this time the
"ince" was distinctly "Prince!" Then it became "Dear Prince," and, turning her head,
she felt hair rippling about her shoulders. She
looked at her little white furry feet. They were
still white, but no longer furry, and a pair of
silver sandals had been fastened upon them by
some magical unseen fingers. Also, they peeped
out now from under the hem of a beautiful silk
dress. The cat hastily got up from the hearth-
rug and took a chair. Minute after minute the
change went on, so that, when the Prince came
home from hunting, he found a perfectly lovely
Princess waiting for him, seated with great
dignity on the most magnificent couch in the
room.

When, in much astonishment, he asked where
she had come from, she told him that her parents

lived far away—as, indeed, they did—but that she herself had often been near to him and watched him—as, indeed, she had. The Prince decided that she was far too beautiful and attractive to be questioned, and rather rashly proposed to her after they had talked together for a very little while. She accepted him instantly; and they were married with all the feastings and rejoicings due to the occasion.

She was a most lovely Princess as she swept about the palace in the golden crown and embroidered train that royal folks wore all day long in those times. You may be sure nobody had the slightest idea that she had once been the castle cat. But, now and then, there was a look in her grey-green eyes that puzzled the Prince. He often thought, too, that she had an oddly slow, soft way of washing her pretty pink little ears. And, one day, he found her, very cautiously, trying to sharpen her nails on the stem of a rose tree in the royal gardens!

Still, he did not suspect, and for a time he was happy enough. But as the weeks went on he found that his Princess, though she continued to charm him by her appearance, was not able to help him in ruling his kingdom. All she really seemed to care for was the petting he gave her, and the nice things she had to eat. Then, too, she spent far too much time asleep on the sofa;

and, when nobody was there, she would even lie down and doze on the rug!

But the Lady with the chariot of doves had by no means forgotten the Princess she had made out of a cat.

One day she came driving along, outside the window, and drew up her white doves upon the sill. Peeping through the casement, she saw the Prince seated upon a couch, trying to persuade his Princess to read out of a wise book. The Princess was yawning, and blinking at a glass of milk which stood on the table. So what do you think the Lady with the doves did?

She put her hand inside the cushions of her chariot and pulled out a *mouse*! Then down on to the carpet she popped the little creature, which instantly squeaked, waved its tail, and scampered off under the very couch on which the Prince and Princess sat!

Down leapt the Princess, her green eyes flashing and all her ten fingers stretched out. Flat on the floor she grovelled, crumpling up her embroidered train and letting her golden crown slide down over her nose. Round and round the room she scrambled on all fours, her arms flung out and her mouth wide open. And at last, to her husband's horror and dismay, she caught the mouse between her teeth and began to shake it backwards and forwards as hard as she could!

Then, all at once, he heard the voice of the Lady on the window-sill, and caught a glimpse of the rosy cloud which floated round the doves and their lovely driver.

"Wretched Princess!" said the Lady, "you had every chance of happiness if you could have changed your nature as you promised! But you have failed miserably. So now——"

She waved her wand, and the Princess (who had killed the mouse by this time) vanished immediately, crown, sandals, train, and all. Instead of his bride running round the room on all fours the Prince beheld his old friend, the castle cat!

And there is not the slightest doubt that it was a great relief to his feelings. For what well-conducted Prince could wish for a wife who sharpened her nails on the rose-trees, slept the whole afternoon on the best sofa, and ran on all fours among the chairs and tables trying to catch a mouse?

THE THREE WISHES

ONE fine morning in early winter a wood-man, who spent nearly all his time fel-ling trees, went out from his little hut, made of pine-logs and roofed with willow, into the leafless forest that spread to his very door. He carried his big axe with him, and, pausing near a fine oak, began to make preparations for cutting it down.

He was marking and measuring and examining the little twigs at the ends of the boughs, when suddenly a gentle sighing shook the tree, and a soft voice spoke to him sadly from the branches.

" Oh, kind sir ! " sighed the voice, " have pity on me ! I have made my winter home in this tree. If you cut it down I shall have nowhere to sleep, and must die in the cold."

The woodman was so surprised that he dropped his axe and nearly cut off his toes.

" Who are you ? " he exclaimed. " I can't see you ! "

" No, because I am a woodland fairy, and you can only see the branches that rock me, the rough bark that clothes me, and the little twigs where, in the spring, I shall shake out my delicate green hair! If you will spare me I will grant you and your wife three wishes. With these wishes you can get anything you like, and make yourselves so rich that neither of you need work any more!"

The woodman at once agreed to leave the tree standing, so that the fairy might sleep beneath its bank until the spring.

Hurrying home, he told his wife what had happened. Then he flung himself into his chair and asked for breakfast.

"There is only porridge!" said the old lady. "But with three wishes we can——"

"Only porridge!" interrupted the woodman. "I wish a good hot string of black-puddings would come tumbling down the chimney——"

He broke off with a jump, and his wife gave a little shriek and dropped the porridge. Down the chimney had popped the biggest, longest, hottest string of black-puddings you ever saw in your life! The woodman's mouth watered as he looked at them.

"Get a plate, wife!" he cried. "Here's a breakfast for a hungry man!"

"Plate!" sneered his wife angrily, "get a plate for yourself! One of our three wishes gone, and nothing but a string of black puddings to show for it! I wish they were hanging to the tip of your silly nose!"

"*Ugh! ugh! ugh!*" shouted the woodman, springing quite a yard across the kitchen. "What's this? What's this?"

He was shaking his head like a terrier with a rat. For, at his wife's words, the whole string of black puddings had jumped off the hearth, and fastened themselves firmly to the tip of his nose.

The woodman raged with anger and fright as he struggled vainly to shake the black puddings from his nose. His wife, terrified out of her wits, brought a big knife to try and chop them away—but they were fairy black puddings, and she could no more cut them off than she could cut off her husband's head. She began to cry and the more she cried, the more bad language the woodman used. However, the black puddings, still steaming hot, remained dangling from the tip of his nose.

He was so upset and excited that he quite forgot that he still had a third wish. But his wife, who was less impulsive, and who, moreover, had no black puddings hanging to *her* nose, remembered it very well. She dried her tears, and begged him to sit in his old armchair and talk the matter over.

"Never mind! Never mind," said she, as

" The whole string of black puddings had jumped
off the hearth, and fastened themselves firmly
to the tip of the woodman's nose."

soothingly as she could. "We'll have a grand house, and keep hens and chickens, and have servants to wait on us as well. We have only to decide how much money to wish for, so that we may be able to live comfortably for the rest of our lives."

"Live comfortably!" screamed her husband. "Who's going to live comfortably with a reeking, dangling, streaming string of black puddings swinging at the end of his nose? I wish to goodness they were up the chimney, where they came from."

Hey, presto! He felt a sort of electric shock in his nose, and, without a sound, the string of black puddings took a flying leap into the fire and disappeared up the chimney. The woodman and his wife were left staring at each other. At last the old husband spoke, rubbing his nose at the same time.

"What's the good of wishing for things?" he said philosophically. "You never know where you are when you've got them. Make a fresh basin of porridge, wife, and we'll have our breakfast."

And that was the end of the Three Wishes given to the woodman and his wife by the fairy who lived in the tree.

THE TWO JARS

TWO jars once stood on a shelf in a house near a river. One was made of china, the other of heavy shining brass, ornamented with handsome designs. The second jar had cost a large sum of money, and its owner was extremely proud of it—a pride which was fully shared by the jar. It gave itself all sorts of airs, and would have puffed itself inside out with conceit if its brass body had not been too hard to change its shape by even the fraction of an inch.

The china vase, for its part, was a modest, sedate little thing in its dress of blue and white. It was ornamented with pictures of men and bridges and storks and pretty drooping willow trees, and it asked for nothing better. But the brass jar imagined that its china companion was always envying it, and looking up to it as a poor person is supposed to look up to his rich relations.

Then, one day, a great storm beat over the country. The river overflowed its banks and came singing into the house. When it surged out again it carried a good deal of the furniture with it ; and, among other things, it swept away the brass and china jars.

How they bobbed, and wobbled, and drifted about in the swirl of the water ! Through what had once been the garden they sailed—through the willows and rushes and down the little sudden waterfalls that appeared so surprisingly where waterfalls had never been before. At last they found themselves close together, being carried side by side down the stream, apparently on their way to sea.

The brass jar, though it was rocking and toppling from side to side, managed to keep its dignity.

" Pray come a little nearer to me," it said, pompously, to the other. " Do not be afraid of annoying me by your closeness ! I will protect you in the alarming circumstances in which we both unexpectedly find ourselves ! "

But the china vase, which, being so much lighter, found it quite easy to keep afloat without assistance, slipped away on the top of a little handy wave.

" You are very good to show such kindness," it said. " But it is kindness that would certainly be the death of me ! If you were to come bumping up against me your heavy brass handles would

Said the china vase, " If you were to come bumping up against me your heavy brass handles
would soon knock a hole in my delicate china
sides."

soon knock a hole in my delicate china sides!
So I pray you, believe that your room is better
than your company!"

And the little china jar disappeared entirely
on the other side of an island of bulrushes.
Lordly companions might be all very well, it
thought, but sometimes their friendship was
likely to end in a serious accident.

THE OAK AND THE REED

AT the edge of a forest there grew a great oak, which was finer than any other oak in the wood. Tall and straight it was, and, however hard the rough winds blew, the oak stood upright, with its head high against the clear blue sky.

At the foot of the oak grew green reeds, for a river flowed close at hand. The winds, that could not bend the oak, swept over the reeds also. But all the reeds bowed before the gale, curtseying deeply as it swept by. So, one day, the oak asked them why it was they were so meek.

One of the reeds answered the great tree softly. "We are not so strong as you are," it said. "We are obliged to bend because we cannot stand upright. The wind is too powerful for us."

"Is that so?" replied the oak. "Then my strength is indeed a thing to be proud of, since I can stand unmoved before the might of a violent gale."

" The great oak asked the reeds why it was
they were so meek."

F*

THE OAK AND THE REED

However, a day or two after, a terrible storm came up over the hills, and swept, like a fierce-winged demon, through the wood. The reeds bent, and bent, and bent again; but the oak, prouder than ever of his strength, spread out his twigs and branches firmly, and refused to bend at all.

Alas for the proud oak! A gust, wilder than any that had gone before, suddenly struck his topmost branches. *Crack! Crack! Crack!* went something under the ground. And down toppled the oak, torn up by the roots in the gale.

The storm passed, but the oak was killed, and could never be set up again. Round about him the reeds were safe and sound. They had been saved by their quiet bending to the great wind, and, when the sun shone on the river again they swayed about the bank, pretty and green and gentle as ever.

THE ELEPHANTS AND THE MOON

IN a great jungle of feathery cedars and gum-scented pines, where big sweet flowers opened at moonrise and closed and died at dawn, lived the elephant-people, lords of this dim and spicy wood. They found good delicious food there; and the streams danced, bright and glancing, among high ferns, giving plenty of water for them to drink. But, after one long hot summer, the rain was late in coming over the distant snow-mountains, and the sparkling streams dried up. So the elephants, very thirsty, went to the King of the herd, and asked him to find water for them somewhere.

"I know of no place where there is water," said the King. "But if you will follow me I will lead you on a voyage of adventure in search of some!"

The elephants, in a long single file, followed their King upon this voyage of adventure. They tramped through villages and rice-fields, tiger-haunted jungles, and great gardens where tea-shrubs grew. And at last they reached a pool where the water bubbled up, clear as crystal, from a spring deep hidden in the earth. With great joy the elephants gathered round it, thrust their trunks deep into the ripples, and, as well as drinking as much as ever they wanted, squirted the water over each other in a glorious shower-bath.

But all round about the spring was a rabbit-warren! And goodness knows how many little soft rabbits were not trampled to death by the large heavy feet of the elephant-people, who did not even see the small furry creatures, and probably would not have minded if they had. So, when the elephants went away until the following evening, the rabbits met together, and, with many sighs and tears, discussed the seriousness of the situation.

"They have gone away now, those great ugly strangers!" said one indignant and unhappy rabbit. "But there is not the slightest doubt that they will come back! In a week's time not a single rabbit will be alive to tell our story!"

An old grandfather rabbit, very grave and sedate, reproved the others for being so faint-hearted.

"Trust to me," said Mr. Grandfather. "I will prevent such a tragedy!"

And he set off to make good his promise, without waiting for anybody to ask him how he was going to do it.

But he was an uncommonly shrewd and clever grandfather-rabbit, and knew every rabbit proverb by heart! He began to repeat these proverbs to himself as he made his way in little low creeping jumps through the thick grass. The first three proverbs did not help him much, for they were all about kings, and serpents, and wicked men. But the fourth proverb was about elephants, and was quite clear and distinct.

"Elephants kill you when they tread upon you," said this wise proverb, which no rabbit had ever attempted to dispute. Mr. Grandfather repeated it once or twice, and then added to himself, "This being so, I will mount upon a rock that is taller than an elephant, and from there I will address the King of the troop!"

No sooner said than done! The elephants, placidly browsing round the base of the rock, suddenly heard a small squeaking voice addressing them. They looked up, and there, above their heads, saw a little creature such as they never remembered to have seen before.

"Who are you?" demanded the King of the elephants, "and where do you come from?"

"Sir," answered the rabbit, making his squeak as impressive and noble as he could. "I am an ambassador from His Majesty the Moon!"

THE ELEPHANTS AND THE MOON

(Was there ever so brave, wonderful, romantic and cunning a rabbit, even in a forest where elephants ramble among feathery cedars and pines ?)

" Declare your errand, my Lord Ambassador," said the King of the elephants, in no wise surprised at receiving a message from His Majesty the Moon.

But the rabbit felt a little nervous at the sight of the ivory gleaming tusks and the royal trunk that waved like a pillar of a temple moving up and down. So, first of all, he hurriedly showed the King that he knew the rules of warfare.

" I must first remind you," squeaked the rabbit, " that ambassadors are sacred folk ! They come for the benefit of the State to which they belong ! They are on no account to be eaten up, or trodden flat, or put to death in any other fashion ! "

" Proceed ! " was all the King said, with a commanding wave of his trunk.

" Certainly ! I will now declare the commands of His Majesty the Moon ! " went on the rabbit. " He told me to say that in driving away and killing the rabbits who are guarding his royal pool you have done a very wrong thing ! For the rabbits are his own bodyguard, and in all the pictures of His Majesty he is shown in a

III

chariot drawn by two antelopes, carrying a rabbit, instead of a sceptre, in his hand!"

Then the King was dreadfully frightened, for he remembered that he had seen just such pictures of His Majesty the Moon. He asked what he had better do, and the rabbit told him to come along to the pool, and make humble apologies to His Majesty, who would be seen seated, trembling with anger, in the middle of the water.

So off set the very small rabbit and the very big elephant to the pond of His Majesty the Moon. And there, sure enough, was the silver reflection of the round and beautiful moon that hung in the dark sky overhead, surrounded by a hundred diamond stars. The King of the elephants gazed at the image gravely. He was too big and slow for his ideas to move very fast, so he never thought of turning up his great head to see the real moon shining in the sky.

As he looked, a little breeze ran over the pool, and the moon in the water began to shiver and shake. The rabbit sat up excitedly.

"See!" he cried, pointing with his dumpy, furry paw. "Did I not tell you? His Majesty is even now trembling with anger because you, and your heavy companions, have crushed so many of the guardians of his pool!"

Then the King of the elephants went down on his big knees before the reflection of the moon,

and humbly begged His Majesty's forgiveness
for the harm which he and the other elephants
had done. After which he led the herd home in a
great hurry, and left the rabbits in safe possession
of their warren round about the clear pool.
And the old grandfather-rabbit added a new
proverb to those that were already collected
for the benefit of his grandchildren :

"Great things may be done by the cleverness
of the little to get the better of the big and
strong."

THE LITTLE BOY AND THE NETTLE

WITH wide big eyes a small boy stood staring at a bank of nettles. He thought they looked harmless green things, yet he had often been told that they could sting him as badly as wasps. He drew a little nearer, and peeped a little more earnestly, wondering where they kept those terrible stings. At last he put out his fat little finger, and, very cautiously, stroked the nettle that was nearest to his hand.

Sting! sting! sting! went the nettle. And "*Ow! Ow! Ow!*" cried the silly little boy. Running home to his mother as fast as he could, he showed her his hand, all swollen and covered with white blisters.

"The horrid nettle has stung me!" he said indignantly. "Yet I only stroked its leaves ever so carefully with the tip of my finger!"

His mother smiled a little as she covered the white blisters with nice cold cream.

"That is the way of nettles!" said she. "They are cunning little green fellows, but great cowards!

" Sting, sting ! sting ! went the nettle.
' *Ow ! Ow ! Ow !* ' cried the silly little boy."

THE LITTLE BOY AND THE NETTLE

If you show you are afraid of them they will sting with all their might. But if you seize hold of them boldly, and crush them in your hand, they won't be able to do you any harm at all. Try this the next time you want to handle a nettle—only you had better not try the same plan with a wasp!"

THE BLACKAMOOR

IN the days when blackamoors were bought and sold as slaves, a white merchant, who had but recently become wealthy, purchased one of these dark-skinned negroes for the first time, and took him home to his wife and family.

"See! I have bought a slave!" he cried triumphantly. "Is he not a magnificent creature—or at least he would be if he were not so dirty! I can't think what his late master was thinking of to allow him to become such a colour! Why he is positively as black as ink!"

He walked round and round the blackamoor, touching him with his fingers here and there. The slave, knowing it was not his business to teach his master, said nothing. Also, as he came from a distant country, he very likely did not know the white man's language.

"Come!" said the proud merchant. "We can't let such neglect continue! We must wash him white!"

So, along with the rest of his family, he set to work to wash the negro white. They armed

" So the merchant set to work to wash the negro white."

themselves with soap, scrubbing brushes, and a pail of hot water apiece. And they rubbed and scrubbed and lathered and doused the poor negro for the greater part of an hour. But he remained as black as ever !

Then they tried other things, such as sand-paper, soda, and household ammonia. And they scrubbed the blackamoor for another hour. But still he was no nearer becoming white than before.

Whether they went on to such terribly strong preparations as salts of lemon and chloride of lime the story does not tell us. But it does tell about the end of the washing-day, which was that the unhappy blackamoor, not being used to spending hours and hours in a lather of suds, caught a most terrible cold in his chest, and very nearly died of it. So the merchant, who had spent one day in giving him the cold, had to spend at least twenty days in curing him ; a lesson that blackamoors cannot change their skins any more than leopards can change their spots.

"What do you think was the first thing that met Mr. Hare's gaze? Why, the sleeping form of Mr. Tortoise, who, with Mr. Fox by his side, was taking a comfortable and well-earned rest."

G*

with great dignity. " We are going to race for honour and glory."

The hare nodded his head from where he sat on the rock, and repeated the words quite gravely.

" For honour and glory ! "

" Oh," said Mr. Fox, rather disappointed. " Then what do you want me to do ? "

" To choose the goal and mark out the course," answered the tortoise, " and the longer and harder the better ! "

Mr. Fox thought the affair was going to be amusing, even if there were no prize. So he sat up on his haunches, looked wisely round the landscape, and finally nodded his head towards the towers of a city miles and miles away.

" You shall race to that city," said he, " and you shall go round by the river on the left, and over the hill on the right, and through the oak-wood in the valley ! I will keep an eye on both of you to see that you race fairly."

He trotted off, glancing back over his shoulder now and then, and showing a good deal of interest in Mr. Hare ! But Mr. Hare was looking superior, and rather contemptuous.

" Good morning to you, Mr. Tortoise," said he. " I'll see you again in a day or two ! "

Off he leapt, slipped quickly and cautiously past Mr. Fox, and bounded gaily in the direction of the city. Mr. Tortoise just waited to say good-bye to his wife and family, and then set out in the same direction.

Mr. Hare galloped merrily for a mile or so, and then, feeling rather tired, looked for a nice spot where he could rest. When he had found one, warm and sweet among the clover, he lay down.

" I can certainly spend the rest of the day here," he said to himself. " In the cool of the evening I will set out again for the city. I shall overtake Mr. Tortoise in a very few minutes ! "

So he settled himself with his nose on his forefeet, and almost immediately fell asleep.

But Mr. Tortoise, under his shell, was more wide-awake than he had ever been in his life. Slowly and surely, slowly and surely, he made his way down to the river on the left and swam through it very easily indeed. Then up the hill on the right he clambered, his funny little feet moving steadily under his shell. Through the oak-wood he crept, making a little slow dark moving patch under the shadows of the trees. And, as evening came on, he saw the spires of the city right in front !

Mr. Hare meanwhile had slept soundly among the clover the whole day long. All at once he woke with a start. The sun had set, and a moon like a crystal ball was hanging right over his head in the sky.

THE HARE AND THE TORTOISE

" Bless my soul, I've overslept myself ! " exclaimed Mr. Hare, leaping to his feet. And off he rushed like the wind.

Down to the river he hurried, and swam straight to the other side—and if you tell me that hares don't swim rivers I can only answer that they do ! Over the hill and through the wood he galloped on his noiseless pads. And at last he, too, saw the spires of the city right in front.

Then he bounded to the gates ; but what do you think was the first thing that met his gaze ? Why, the sleeping form of Mr. Tortoise, who, with Mr. Fox by his side, was taking a comfortable and well-earned rest !

" Ah-ha ! " cried Mr. Fox, as Mr. Hare sat down in the moonlight and shook his long ears angrily. " You are a quick runner, Mr. Hare, as nobody knows better than myself ! But if quick runners want to win a race with slow runners, *they mustn't lie down and go to sleep on the way !* "

THE DOG IN THE MANGER

ONCE, a long time ago, there lived a little dog who has been talked about for hundreds of years as the most selfish little dog in the world. The story told of him is that, one evening, he found his way into a cow-shed, and jumped into a manger that was filled with sweet fragrant hay, all ready for the cow's supper. There he curled himself up and went to sleep.

By and by the cattle came pacing in, one by one, and their breath, in the twilight, was as sweet as the hay itself. They stood in a row in front of the long manger, and put their cool, wet mouths into the hay. But up jumped the little dog from behind one of the loosened trusses, and ran from end to end of the manger, snapping at every cow's nose! The cows were so startled that they threw up their horned heads and sprang back; while the naughty little dog yapped and snarled and snapped, running backwards and forwards, as fast as it could, along the heaped-up hay.

THE DOG IN THE MANGER

Whenever a cow put its head near the manger, the dog tried to bite the poor thing. So that all the cattle " mooed " sadly, and said to each other :

" Was there ever the like of this ? The little dog cannot possibly eat the hay himself, for he lives on biscuits and bones ! Yet he will not let us poor cows come near it, though he knows we are longing for our supper. Surely he is the most selfish little dog in the wide world."

And he was ! That is why he has been called " the dog in the manger " ever since !

THE OWL AND THE EAGLE'S DAUGHTER

A YOUNG owl was flying through the woods on a beautiful moonlit night, calling out his strange *tu-whoo-tu-whoo-oo-oo !* " As he flew he came to a river, full of pools that were both clear and deep. The owl hung over one of these pools on his great soft wings, looking for little fishes. And if you don't believe that owls eat little fishes, you can spend the next moonlight night alongside just such a river as the one in this story, and you will know better what to believe and what not to believe !

Well, the owl saw no fishes, but he saw something he had never seen before—the reflection of himself. And he hung over it as pleased as any flower on the bank, lost in admiration of his own appearance.

" What a face ! What a figure ! " he cried, in excited little hoots. " Never could I have believed in such beauty if I had not seen it for myself ! Those eyes—how bright and brown ! That beak—how delicately curved ! And oh !

what a becoming wreath of dainty white and black feathers I wear round my face ! Truly, I am a handsome and attractive young owl ! I should like to marry the eagle's daughter ! "

He sailed away from the moonlit pool, full of this new idea. But the eagle lived a long way off, in a high mountain, and Mr. Owl had not much chance of becoming acquainted with him. So, next morning, the young dandy put his head out of his ivy bush and called to his friend Mr. Crow, who was preparing for a day's hunting.

" Mr. Crow ! Mr. Crow ! " he cried, " will you do me a favour ? "

Mr. Crow paused. He was a carrion crow, and was quite as fond of mice and little rabbits as was Mr. Owl. In the same way, he made his home in the thick woods. But he had stronger wings than the owl and could fly a long way in the daylight.

So Mr. Owl explained that, finding he was so handsome, he had made up his mind to marry the eagle's daughter. And he begged Mr. Crow to carry his compliments to the King of the birds, and to ask for the hand of the young lady in marriage. " For," said he, " the eagle is not very well acquainted with me, owing to my habit of remaining at home all day and only going abroad at night. But he knows you very well, and will no doubt listen to you when you describe the young and handsome creature who desires to marry his daughter."

Mr. Crow consented to do this, and made his way to the home of the golden eagles, up in the high mountains. There, on a big crag, sat the King of the birds, his fierce gaze fixed on the distance, his great claws gripping the edge of the stone. Just below was his nest of sticks ; and in the nest were his three soft, downy-grey daughters, the Royal Family of the moment.

The crow bobbed his dark head humbly to King Eagle, and explained his errand.

" Down in the forest far below your Majesty's palace lives an owl," said the carrion crow. " He is exceedingly handsome, and remarkably wise. He begs me to ask for the hand of one of the Princesses in marriage."

The Eagle King scowled over his great beak for a minute. Then he broke into little sharp shrieks of laughter.

" What ! An owl marry an eagle's daughter ! " cried he. " A pretty union ! Pray what can he offer her ? "

" He can offer her a home in an ivy-bush, and plenty of mice and young rabbits to eat."

" Ivy-bush ! Mice ! Rabbits ! " snorted the eagle. " A fine home and fine fare for a Princess ! But let us put your young Mr. Owl upon his mettle. Tell him to meet me at noon in the

" Over his head all the time the owl heard the
mocking cries of the great eagle."

high skies, under the golden rays of the sun. I will discuss this marriage with him there, but nowhere else."

The eagle spread his enormous wings and sailed off into the blue, and the carrion crow went back to the young owl.

"Well?" said the owl, poking his head carefully out of his dark, comfortable bush. "What does King Eagle say?"

Mr. Crow gave him the eagle's message, and looked up into the hot blue sky above the cool wood.

"He is there, now," said the crow, "flying round and round in a circle, waiting for you!"

"Oh, is he?" answered the owl rather ruefully. Then, with a little defiant hoot, he hopped out of his ivy-bush, blinking hard.

"Well, I suppose I must fly up to him," he said. "Good morning, Mr. Crow. I shall come back engaged to the eagle's daughter!"

Then up into the air rose Mr. Owl, and high above the trees he flew. But, oh, how strange and scorching hot and blinding he found the midday skies. Never before had he felt the sun's rays so hot on his dark, noiseless wings. Never before had he opened his brown eyes, which he thought so beautiful, to the noontide glare. Exhausted and half-blinded, he struggled on; while over his head, all the time, he heard the mocking cries of the great eagle, as the magnificent bird sailed easily round and round in the sunshine, and opened his brilliant eyes fully to the radiant light.

For a long time the owl tried to reach the eagle, but at last he could struggle no longer. Down, down, down, he dropped, back to his ivy-bush in the wood. With a little hoot of thankfulness, he crept into his cosy hole, a sadder and a wiser bird.

"Eagle's daughter!" he panted to himself. "No eagle's daughter for me, now that I know the family habits! Fancy having a wife who wanted to fly round and round for hours in the burning sun! I will marry a sensible downy little owl like myself, who will come hooting and hunting with me o' nights, among the shadows and the cool, glimmering dews!"

As for the eagle he flew home, still laughing to himself mockingly.

"My dear," he said to his eldest daughter, as he handed her a nice young grouse. "A funny little fellow called an owl wanted to marry you as soon as you grew up. But I flatter myself that I have taught him to keep his place!"

THE FOX AND THE GRAPES

WOULD you like to know why people sometimes laugh and say to each other, "Sour grapes"?

Well, they are thinking of the story of a hungry fox who lived in a land so sunny that the grapes ripened on vines in the open air. One evening this fox set off a-hunting, as foxes do, and presently came to a rich man's garden, full of roses for sweet scents and gay colours, and dark cypress trees for cool shade. Better than any of these, to the fox's mind, however, was a high trellis covered with vines. And among the green vine-leaves hung bunches of purple grapes.

"I will have some of those grapes for my supper," said the fox to himself. So he crouched down, and then made a flying leap, up from the ground, at the grapes.

But, though all his four pads were in the air at once, he landed back on the pathway without having reached even the lowest bunch that hung on the vine above his head. He was naturally very much disappointed and annoyed.

H

" The fox leaped again and again at the sweet, ripe, purple grapes."

THE FOX AND THE GRAPES

He was a persevering fox, however, and his mouth was still watering for the grapes. So he leaped again and again until, at last, he was so tired that he could not jump more than four inches from the ground. Then he lifted his head, and barked at the sweet, ripe, purple grapes.

" Nasty sour things you are," he snarled contemptuously. " I wouldn't eat you if you fell right off the branches of the vine into my mouth ! Who cares for sour grapes ? "

And off he went, snarling and yarling, in search of something else for supper, leaving the delicious grapes to be eaten by the man who owned the beautiful garden.

So, now that you have heard this story of the fox, you will know what people mean when they laugh and say, " Sour grapes."

THE FOX AND THE COCK

ALL through the history of the world no animals have done such clever things as the foxes. But this is the tale of a cock who was cleverer still.

The cock belonged to the people of a big city, and they thought the world of it, for it always gave them warning when the sun was going to rise. They would have overslept themselves time and time again had it not been for the cock. They kept him in a special little house in a field, where they had kept his father before him. And not only his father, but his grandfather, and his great grandfather, and all his other direct ancestors, for the family was as old as the city itself.

One day, through the hedge that surrounded the field, came creeping a sly red fox. The cock hopped up on to a little mound to get out of the visitor's way, but the fox sat down and began to talk to him, as soft as butter and as sweet as sugar.

" Admirable, handsome, bright-eyed, silver-

" 'Never was there such a musical voice!' went on Mr. Fox. 'To hear him sing "Cock-a-doodle-doo" you would think that all the nightingales of the district were having a concert!'"

tongued Mr. Cock," said he. " I knew your father in days gone by. Ah! he was a wonderful old cock! I could tell you many a story of the things he did! "

The cock put his head on one side, and blinked his bright eyes complacently.

" His voice, too! " went on Mr. Fox. " Never was there such a musical voice! To hear him sing 'Cock-a-doodle-doo' you would think that all the nightingales of the district were having a concert! "

He paused a moment, then said under his breath!

" What would I not give to hear for myself if you have such a voice as your father! "

There was silence for a second. Then, " *Cock-a-doodle-doo-oo-oo!* " went the cock on the mound, his mouth wide open and his eyes tightly shut. " *Cock-a-doodle-doodle-doodle-dud-dud-squawk!* "

He choked shrilly over the last *doodle*, and ended up with a terrible, gurgling *squawk*. For the fox had leapt on to the mound, seized him in his mouth, and was running away with him!

" *Squawk! Squawk! Squawk!* " screamed the cock again; so that the people in the city, hearing him, called to each other in dismay.

" Do you hear that? A fox is running away with our cock! "

But, by this time, the cock was pulling himself

together, for he was a very clever old cock. He stopped "squawking," and now it was his turn to talk as soft as butter, and as sweet as sugar.

"My lord," said he to the fox, cunningly, "Do you know what the people of the city are saying? They are calling to each other that you are carrying off their cock! Was ever such a mistake made? It is to you I belong, my lord! I have never been the property of these people! You have always possessed me and, naturally, have at last come to claim your own. Open your lordly mouth, my lord, and tell the foolish people that I am yours!"

Mr. Fox's jaws opened wide. He put his head over his shoulder, and called out grandly to the people who were running after him:

"This is my cock, good folks. He says so himself!"

Then he shut his mouth again as quickly as possible, but there was no cock there now! As soon as Mr. Fox had opened his jaws, Mr. Cock had flown out of them and perched himself, crowing triumphantly, at the top of a tall tree.

"What lies you are telling!" cried the cock, quite forgetting the lies he had told himself. "I do not belong to you and never did! I belong to the people of the city, and they will soon arrive at the foot of the tree and take me safely home in a bag!"

Surely enough, they did. And, while Mr. Cock was chuckling and crowing contentedly as he was carried home in the bag, Mr. Fox was— what do you think Mr. Fox was doing?

Well, he was hitting his own mouth hard against the ground, and scolding it at the same time.

"You foolish mouth!" said he, "don't you know your own business? There is a time to talk, but there is also a time to eat! You spent your breath in words when, if you had had any sense, you would have spent it in swallowing the cock! Oh! silly mouth! I will teach you sense!"

And no doubt Mr. Fox's silly mouth learnt the lesson and succeeded, in future, in doing the right thing at the right time. As for Mr. Cock, he never forgot that to shut your eyes and crow when a fox is talking to you is certain to end in serious trouble.

THE MAN AND THE SATYR

THIS happened in the days when satyrs walked among the trees in the woods.

They were strange creatures who long ago lived in the land of witches and fairies and wizards. In some ways they were like tall wild men, but they had hooves instead of feet, and little curly horns grew out of their small pricked-up ears. Men were generally afraid of them; but they were too fleet and wild to be afraid of men, though they kept to themselves in the forest, laughing, singing, playing flutes, and drinking sweet honeyed wine.

Once, however, a man and a satyr made friends. It was in winter. The satyr had lost his companions and had been wandering alone through the snow. He came across the man's hut in the forest, and the man saw him and invited him inside. The satyr stalked in very gladly, and sat down by the fire, warming his great hooves and strange knees, that were covered with hair like a goat's.

The man, however, who was busily preparing a

meal, was not so close to the fire, and, by and by, put his fingers to his mouth and blew on them. The satyr, watching him, wondered why he did this.

"You blow on your fingers, sir," said he politely. "Pray can you tell me the reason?"

"To be sure," answered the man, quite as polite as the satyr. "They are cold and I do it to warm them."

The satyr thought this strange. He wondered if the man kept a fire inside him. However, he went on warming his own fingers in what he considered a much wiser fashion, and said nothing.

Presently the man, having set out his clean plates and dishes, took a pan of porridge from the fire and poured it into a basin. Then he invited the satyr to draw to the table and eat. Very sedately, the great goat-like creature seated himself and was duly helped to the porridge.

But the porridge was exceedingly hot. The satyr waited for it to cool, as was wise. The man, however, took up a spoonful, and blew on it with all his might, just as he had blown on his fingers.

"Pray, good sir," said the satyr, "will you tell me, now, why you blow upon the porridge?"

"To be sure," replied the man. "I do it to cool it!"

The satyr pushed aside his plate and stood up,

staring at the man in dismay. Then he began to move hurriedly towards the door.

"Why are you going?" asked the man. "Don't you want anything to eat?"

"I'm going because I daren't stay!" answered the satyr, thoroughly frightened. "I always thought men were strange animals, but I never thought to meet one who could first blow hot and then blow cold out of the very same mouth!"

THE CROW AND THE SNAKE

IN a high fork of a big tree a pair of crows had lived for a long time, making a new nest every spring and doing their best to bring up a new family. But each year the poor little crows, almost as soon as they had kicked and struggled their way out of the eggs, were eaten up by a great black snake. Family after family disappeared down the hungry snake's ugly throat; and as his own mansion was in a hollow at the foot of the tree, he had every opportunity of breaking into Mr. and Mrs. Crow's residence at the top.

At last Mrs. Crow lost her patience, as well she might.

"My dear," she said to her husband, "I am tired of laying nice smooth warm eggs, and sitting tightly on the top of them for two or three weeks, only to have my nestlings eaten up by that greedy, cruel Mr. Snake down in the basement of our family property. I cannot kill him myself, nor apparently can you! So I mean to use my wits to save our race from entire destruction ! ''

" What do you mean to do, my dear ? " asked Mr. Crow humbly, for he felt that he, himself, must be in some way to blame.

" You shall see," replied Mrs. Crow. And as at the moment the King's son came along with one or two courtiers to bathe in the river, she flew on to a stump among the reeds and waited.

The King's son took off his embroidered clothes, his jewelled chains, and his exquisite stockings, and laid them carefully upon the bank before he plunged into the cool, rippling river, with a courtier on either side of him. Down from her stump hopped Mrs. Crow on to the heap of beautiful garments, seized a magnificent golden bracelet in her beak, and popped it, with all haste, into the hole of the snake, who was away at the moment, probably eating up some other crow's family. Then she flew back to her nest with a "caw" of satisfaction, and laid an egg as quickly as she could.

The Prince came out of the river, dried himself, and started to dress again. In a few minutes he missed the bracelet. Very angry at his loss, he told his courtiers that he was not going home until they had found it ; so they began to search breathlessly among the reeds and rushes, declaring

" Mrs. Crow seized a magnificent golden bracelet
in her beak, and popped it, with all haste,
into the hole of the snake, who was away
at the moment."

that, as it could not have walked away by itself, some thief had certainly stolen it.

Meanwhile, Mr. Snake came back to his hole and curled up for a nap. One of the courtiers drew near to the big tree, and peeped into the hollow of the trunk. There he saw the big, black, ugly snake, fast asleep on top of the golden bracelet, only a small part of which was showing.

" Sire ! Sire ! " he called to the Prince. " Here is the thief ! A black snake has stolen your bracelet and is curled up, asleep, on top of it ! "

The other courtier came running up, and the two between them soon killed the snake and recovered the golden bracelet. Then they went home with the delighted Prince—and clever Mrs. Crow, in the tree-top, laid another egg immediately.

" My dear," she cawed to her husband, " you need have no further anxiety. *This* year we shall certainly bring up what I hope will be a large and flourishing family ! "

THE BEE AND THE DOVE

A LITTLE hairy golden-brown bee and a snow-white dove once had a great admiration for each other. They did not speak the same language, nor do the same things, but both loved the sunshine, the clear windless skies of summer, and the green shelter of the woods. So, when the dove, floating in the sky, heard a humming below in the heather, she would think, " There is that good, industrious little chap, the golden-brown bee ! " While the bee would glance up and hum to himself, " There goes the beautiful white dove. How I wish I could tell her all the lovely things I think about her ! "

One day the dove was resting in a willow-tree, smoothing her shining feathers, when suddenly her bright eyes caught sight of something in the water of the stream below her—something small, and dark, and struggling with drenched wings and tiny sodden feet. It was the poor little bee, who had fallen into the river from a wild rose bush on the bank. Down flew the dove, making loud " coo's " of encouragement.

" Down flew the dove, making loud ' coo's ' of
encouragement to the poor little bee."

THE BEE AND THE DOVE

And in her beak she carried a willow-leaf, which she had plucked the moment she became aware of the accident.

She dropped the leaf into the brook and, to the bee, it looked like a great life-boat that bobbed alongside in the raging waves and roaring water-falls made by the ripples. He struggled on board, thankfully and breathlessly ; and the dove, with her wings, made a little breeze that wafted the leaf-boat to land. The bee scrambled ashore, and shook the water from his back. Then he sat rubbing his little legs together, and spreading out his gauzy wings in the sunshine, thinking what a terrifying tale of shipwreck, and wild waters, and tempest, he would have for his friends when he got home.

Meanwhile, the dove flew back to the willow-tree and sat there, cooing contentedly. As she cooed a man came round the corner and heard her. He looked up, and his eyes grew eager. Sitting down under the tree, he opened a large bag that he carried, and began to spread some twigs with sticky stuff which he took out of a bottle. Meanwhile the pretty dove put her head under her wing and went to sleep.

But the bee, drying itself on a honeysuckle flower, was wide-awake and watchful. He saw the man fix the sticky twigs in the ground so that they looked like little dead branches of fir.

THE BEE AND THE DOVE

Then, in the middle of them, this dreadful person began to sprinkle a handful of corn. And the bee knew instantly that a trap was being set for the pretty white dove who had rescued him from drowning.

All the time the dove remained asleep.

The bee buzzed loudly, but could not wake her. Besides, even if he had roused her, she would not have known what the buzzing meant. But the bee was perfectly determined to save the dove from the trap, just as the dove had saved him from the river. So he stole up to the man and gave him a sharp sting on the foot.

Up jumped the man with a loud exclamation. Down fell the trap of sticky twigs! And, frightened by the noise, away flew the startled dove! The man stood, rubbing his foot, and saying all sorts of dreadful things about bees in general. But the good and grateful little fellow who had stung him did not care a jot for the man's remarks. He flew off after the dove on dry gauzy wings, humming to himself!

"*Buzz! Buzz! Buzz!* I am only a little brown insect, and the dove is a big, beautiful, shining bird! But I was able to save her life just as cleverly as she was able to save mine. *Buzz! Buzz!* What a lovely day it is and how jolly to be alive! *Buzz! Buzz! Buzz!*"

THE COUNTRY MOUSE AND THE TOWN MOUSE

A LITTLE country mouse lived in a hole under the stones of a wall, where he stored up all sorts of food for himself and his wife. Every autumn he collected wheat and barley from the fields of grain, berries from the hawthorns, and acorns from the oaks. Altogether, he considered that he lived like a prince; and, one day, he sent an invitation to a town mouse, to come and pay him a visit. The town mouse was a close relation of the country mouse, as anybody could see by the length of their tails. With great pride and pleasure the country mouse showed off his sons and daughters, and brought out all the best things from his larder. As well as the barley and acorns and berries, there were crab-apples and sweet white nuts. But the town mouse looked down his whiskers at the food with an air of condescension, and only nibbled at it languidly, while the country mouse and his wife and children made a hearty meal.

" Oh, my good cousin ! " exclaimed the town

" 'Oh, my good cousin!' exclaimed the Town
Mouse at last. 'Is it possible that you are
contented with such food as this, year in,
year out?'"

" 'It is very good food!' said Mrs. Country Mouse,
rather annoyed."

I*

mouse at last. "Is it possible that you are contented with such food as this, year in, year out?"

"It is very good food!" said Mrs. Country Mouse, rather annoyed. "What fault have you to find with it? My husband worked hard to get it, and I am sure no mouse in the world has a better larder than mine!"

"Dear madam," answered Mr. Town Mouse, "I can see it is excellent, *for the country*. But have you thought how much easier and even cheaper your housekeeping would be in the town?"

"No, I haven't," said Mrs. Country Mouse in a huff. And she whisked away all that was left of the nuts and berries and put them safely aside for the morrow.

But her husband began to ask questions about town life. And, at last, when his cousin went away, it was with an understanding that Mr. Country Mouse should return the visit of Mr. Town Mouse at the very first opportunity.

So, one evening, the country mouse trotted off, his fur nicely brushed, and his paws and tail tidy and clean. The town mouse met him just outside the big city, and warned him at once that he must be careful not to let anybody see him. Very cautiously, the two crept together into the great house where Mr. Town Mouse had taken up his quarters. He led his cousin down long corridors carpeted with velvet, and carefully boarded up under white and gold paint. However, the town mouse had found one tiny hole where he could creep behind the skirting-board, into which hole he escorted his guest. And by and by they came out near a fireplace in a great banqueting-hall, where the chairs were covered with purple satin, and the table was spread with a white lace-edged cloth.

On to this table hopped Mr. Town Mouse, and his country cousin followed. Oh, such fine dishes they saw, and such gleaming gold and silver plates! On the dishes were set out all kinds of dainties for a great feast—plum-puddings and game-pies, and jellies and creams, and roast chickens, and pine-apple preserves. Mr. Country Mouse stared round in amazement. His mouth watered, and he did not know where to begin.

"Try that boiled ham," suggested Mr. Town Mouse, as he took a seat upon the game-pie. "The cook here always boils her hams in champagne!"

Mr. Country Mouse ran delicately up the crumby side of the ham. He was just going to begin his feast when the door burst open and a party of gay people came laughing into the room. With a squeak and a whisk of his long tail, Mr. Town Mouse disappeared into the hole behind the fireplace, and his visitor rushed, full tilt, after him.

" Keep quite still," whispered the town mouse, " or they will know we are here, and never rest till they kill us."

So, peeping out of the hole, they watched the laughing, talking people eat up most of the good things. But Mr. Town Mouse assured Mr. Country Mouse that there would be plenty left. Mr. Country Mouse, however, was beginning to think that he would rather be master in his own house than a stowaway in somebody else's.

After what seemed a long time the noisy people stopped eating and went away. Then the two mice crept out, ran up the table-cloth, and started to nibble the remains of the feast. No sooner had they begun again on what was left of the boiled ham and the game-pie than, once more, the door opened, and a footman came in with a couple of terriers.

" *Houp! Houp! Mice!* " shouted the footman. " At 'em, Vixen! At 'em, Snarley-yow!"

But the mice had whisked behind the fireplace in a trice, and not even a flicker of their tails could be seen. For a long time, Vixen and Snarleyyow yelped and scratched at the hole. At last they gave it up, and the servant cleared the table and took the fussing, yapping dogs away.

" These terrible creatures have gone, and I am going too!" said Mr. Country Mouse, still pale with fright. "Fine food is all very well, cousin, but one still goes hungry if one is not allowed to eat it! Give me barleycorns and safety rather than game-pies and incessant runs for your life! Good-bye, my friend, I'm off."

And, shaking his head wisely, he pattered home to preach lessons of contentment to his wife and family.

THE COMMITTEE OF MICE

NEAR to a great pond there once stood an old mill, so old that its walls hid dozens and dozens of bright-eyed, long-tailed mice. They and their forefathers had lived there for two or three hundred years, and nobody had interfered very much with them. Then, one day, a young miller came along, who was always striding about the mill, looking to see if everything was right with the grain. He soon found out that a good many things were wrong, —and the worst of all the wrong things was the quantity of mice. The mice were so used to thinking that the mill belonged to them that they positively made nests among the wheat, in which they brought up large and hungry families. The energetic young miller grunted once or twice, and then walked off quickly. In an hour or two he came back with a bag— and out of the bag he dumped on the floor an enormous green-eyed cat !

The cat sat in the middle of the grain, washing her face, while all the mice ran hurriedly to the next storey, taking their children with them. Until the evening came the cat dozed placidly, waking up to wash her face at intervals. Then, when twilight fell over the granary, she stood up, stuck her claws into the floor, yawned, arched her back, and set off through the mill on a hunting expedition, which was so successful that she caught and ate quite half a dozen of the fattest mice in the building.

The next night the same thing happened—and the next—and the next. Wherever they tried to hide themselves, at least six or seven mice were caught by the green-eyed, silent-footed cat. And the worst feature of the business was that nobody had the slightest idea when to expect her. She came and went as silently as the moonlight or twilight in which she loved to hunt. The mice only knew that she had arrived when they saw the two shining green danger-signals that were her eyes.

At last, when every family in the mill was in mourning, they asked the cleverest citizens of Mouse-Town to hold a committee-meeting, and discuss the best way of avoiding their terrible enemy, the cat. So all the wise mice assembled ; and I have no doubt they wore crêpe bows on their tails, and carried two pocket-handkerchiefs apiece.

Well, they began to talk the matter over, and soon decided that if only they could hear the cat coming, it would be quite easy to get out of her way. The difficulty was to contrive some sound which would give them warning that she was creeping about the mill with her velvet slippers on her paws. At last one very brilliant young mouse stood up, and waved his tail to command silence.

"I have an idea!" said he. "When those strange beings who are called men want to warn the countryside of anything, they always send somebody along with a big bell. Now, if the cat wore such a bell round her neck, it would ring every time she moved, and we should all know that she was on her way to eat us up. What I suggest, then, is that we should tie a large bell, with a piece of string, round the neck of the cat!"

He looked about for applause, and the mice clapped their tiny paws together as hard as they could. They thought the plan excellent, and, one after another, they stood up and made speeches about it. Three of them spoke at great length about the size of the bell, and whether it should be made of tin or of brass. A fourth declared that so clever an idea could only properly be carried out in silver, or even gold. As for the string, said a fifth, blue or pink ribbon was the correct material with which the bell should be tied round the cat's neck.

THE COMMITTEE OF MICE

Quite half a dozen mice sprang up to argue eagerly about string, ribbon, and bell. All these matters had at last to be put to the vote, and the mice dropped their votes, importantly, into a bag carried round by the secretary and handed, with due ceremony, to the chairman. To finish up with, a vote of thanks was proposed to the brilliant young mouse who had first thought of it all; and this vote, after being proposed, was seconded and carried without a word of objection.

The clever young mouse stood up again, and began to say how pleased·he was with the vote of thanks. As he was speaking, however, a quiet, old, grey mouse who had been sitting silently in his corner, stroking his whiskers, looked up and said thoughtfully:

" Yes, the idea is excellent, and the pink ribbon and the silver bell will do splendidly. *But where is the mouse who is going to tie the bell round the neck of the cat ?* "

The committee-meeting became suddenly silent, and the clever young mouse sat down in a hurry.

" Oh—I—I, well, *I* am engaged to be married ! " said he, as if that was reason enough for not offering to tie the bell to the cat. " My honourable friend on my right——"

" I *am* married ! " squeaked his honourable friend on the right, " and, what's more, my

" The cat caught and ate quite half a dozen
of the fattest mice in the building."

wife is sitting up for me! I must hurry home
—I had no idea it was so late!"

Off he went, full patter, and then the chairman stood up, arm-in-arm with the secretary.

"*Hem!*" said he, "*Hem!* I declare the
meeting over! My friend the secretary will call
another in a few weeks' time. Good afternoon,
gentlemen! Good afternoon!"

And off he hurried, still arm-in-arm with the
secretary, who was as anxious as the chairman
that the meeting should be quickly broken up.
So, as there was neither the secretary to take
notes, nor the chairman to keep order, all the
other mice shook paws with each other, and
strolled carelessly away, humming little songs
under their breath. At last there was nobody
left but the old, quiet, grey mouse, who still sat
there stroking his whiskers, and murmuring to
himself:

"A very good idea! A *ve-ry* good idea! But
where is the mouse who is going to tie the bell
round the neck of the cat?"

THE SHEPHERD WITH THE FLUTE

LONG ago there lived a shepherd who played the flute more beautifully than it has ever been played before or since. His name was Thyrsis, so we are told, and he was in love with a shepherdess, who was called Annette. Naturally, being in love, he was always trying to show Annette what a wonderful fellow he was. He would write verses to her, and sing songs, and tell her stories of the wild beasts that would come dancing to him out of the forest when they heard the exquisite strains of his flute.

Annette was not quite sure whether she believed him or not. One day she came to him and told him she was going fishing ; so Thyrsis went along with her. Annette had a rod, and a line, and flies to catch the fishes, and a basket to fill with those that she caught. Thyrsis, more determined than ever to show her what a very wonderful fellow he was, carried only his flute.

" You will see what you can do with your rod and line," said he. " But, if you don't manage to catch anything, you can look to me and my flute! I, who have charmed lions and tigers, elephants and buffaloes, into dancing and leaping to my music, shall certainly be able to charm the little fishes on to your line and hook!"

Annette tossed her head saucily, and they walked on till they reached the brook. It must have been one of the prettiest brooks in the world, for it flowed through a meadow golden with buttercups, and under thorn-trees white with may. There Annette stood on the bank among the cowslips and forget-me-nots, and fished with all her might. But Thyrsis only wandered up and down and sang sentimentally in the intervals of piping upon his wonderful flute.

He was singing about Annette to the little fishes in the stream!

"Oh! you nice little silver fishes!" he sang. "Do you know who is standing among the cowslips, throwing flies? It is Annette,—pretty Annette, darling Annette, Annette the sweetest girl in the world! No nymph in her cave of blue water is half so beautiful as Annette under the blue sky! And she *loves* little fishes! It is only to men that she is unkind, for she will not marry!" (This he sang very loudly, casting languishing eyes at Annette, who was for ever refusing his proposals.) "If you will only trust her, you will soon find out how kind she is! She has made a sweet little pond to put you in, as clear as diamonds, planted with lilies, and shaded by cool green trees!" (this must have been a shocking fib on the part of Thyrsis; he certainly knew that Annette wanted the fish for supper). "Come, then, little fishes! Come to Annette among the cowslips on the bank!"

But not a single fish put up its little silver nose out of the water. On the contrary, they were frightened by the noise, and hid themselves at the bottom of the stream. So for the whole day Thyrsis sang, and Annette fished, in vain.

At last evening fell, and Thyrsis was in despair. He had been sure the fishes would come dancing and leaping to his songs and music. Annette, by this time, was very cross. She kept making little sounds of contempt, and pouting with her pretty lips that were as red as cherries. Thyrsis felt that all chance of her ever accepting him was at an end. So he did what he had very much better have done at the beginning—ran home and brought back a large net, which he flung among the deaf and dumb fishes.

Upstream he ran, dragging the net after him. Then, as soon as he reached Annette's side, he pulled the net out of the river and threw it at her feet. Behold, not only was it full of fishes, but the fishes were dancing and leaping with all their might, doing their very best to jump out of the net into the stream again!

THE SHEPHERD WITH THE FLUTE

" See ! they *are* dancing ! They are dancing as gracefully as fishes can manage to dance," cried Thyrsis, in great excitement. " Oh ! the silly creatures ! Never have I known anything so absurd ! "

He shook his forefinger at the fishes, looking at Annette out of the corners of his eyes.

" You foolish fishes ! " said he, with great gravity. " All the time I played and sang you never gave a single hop or skip ! And now that I have stopped you are dancing with all your might. Was ever anything in creation so ridiculous as fishes ? "

All the time that he lectured the fishes, he was peeping at Annette out of the corners of his eyes, desperately afraid less she should not think him a wonderful fellow, after all, and should go on laughing at his tales about the dancing elephants and tigers. But what did Annette care ? She only wanted plenty of fishes, whether they danced at the wrong time or the right ! So she filled her basket as quickly as possible, and went home with Thyrsis in quite a good temper, wondering why in the world he could not have thrown a net into the river a little sooner, instead of just singing songs among the buttercups, and playing tunes, upon his flute, on the bank.

And, on the whole, I think Annette's ideas on the matter were right.

THE FOX AND THE STORK

IN a burrow made by an enormous family of
rabbits there lived an alert little fox. He
had taken a fancy to the rabbits' home when
he was quite a youngster, and he had got possession by the simple plan of eating all the rabbits
up! He made a most comfortable house of it,
furnished it with all sorts of things—most of
them stolen. And now he lived there quite
alone, sleeping through the day and hunting
through the night.

One early morning this busy little fox was
trotting home with a dead hare in his mouth,
when he saw a big white bird solemnly stalking
through the river-reeds on legs that were just
like stilts. The big bird bowed to him—for
they were acquaintances—and the fox suddenly
burst out laughing. However, as he laughed
into the furry coat of the hare, the big bird did
not hear him. Mr. Fox was thinking how silly
the other looked, with his long legs and his neck
that was even longer. It suddenly occurred to
the mischievous little gentleman to play a joke

" Every time the stork pulled up a frog he invited the fox to do the same."

K*

on this absurd bird ; so he put the hare carefully down and spoke :

" Good evening, Mr. Stork ! Have you had good hunting ? "

" Fair ! Fair ! " replied the stork. " But the frogs here are getting cautious and difficult to find."

The bird glanced at the hare. He would have enjoyed a few mouthfuls of it very much.

" Come to dinner with me this evening," said the fox graciously. " You shall see the most excellent dish of hare you ever saw in your life."

Mr. Stork accepted the invitation as politely as it was given, and Mr. Fox trotted off again with the hare. When he reached his burrow he began to make arrangements for his visitor. All the time he was laughing silently ; and, when he curled himself up for his long day's nap, he went on chuckling even in his sleep.

At twilight Mr. Stork arrived at Mr. Fox's house. As he could not, of course, get into the burrow, his host prepared to set the supper in the bracken, just outside. He laid the table and put out the plates. Then he disappeared into the burrow for a minute, and came back carrying a large dish, which smelt most deliciously. He set it down and invited Mr. Stork to begin.

But what do you think that mischief-loving

little fox had done ? He had made all the hare into hare-soup !

Poor Mr. Stork ! He stuck his long bill into the soup, and dabbled about, but of course he could not manage to eat it, except by the tiniest mouthfuls, not worth mentioning. Meanwhile Mr. Fox lapped up plateful after plateful, urging Mr. Stork all the time to take his share. But when the meal was over Mr. Stork was as hungry as he had been before it began. He was a proud bird, however, and hid his disappointment and disgust.

"A very excellent dish of hare !" he said condescendingly. "I hardly like to venture to return your hospitality, but, if you will dine with me to-morrow, I will show you a frog stew that will, I hope, be nearly as good."

Mr. Fox accepted the invitation, for he was rather fond of frogs. The next evening he brushed his coat, smoothed his whiskers, and set out to dine with the stork. He found his host ready to welcome him at the edge of the reeds.

"Pray come in ! Pray come in !" said Mr. Stork, leading the way into the bulrushes. "Our little meal is quite ready. I am only sorry I have no plates ! But we can eat out of the same dish quite comfortably."

He waved a claw in the direction of the afore-said dish. But what do you think he had used for the delicious frog-stew ? Why, nothing but a big jar, with a neck as long as his own, out of which came a smell quite as appetizing as the smell of last night's hare-soup.

" Pray help yourself ! " Mr. Stork cried genially to his visitor. " You will find that the stew is done to perfection ! "

He stuck his long neck down to the bottom of the jar and brought up a big frog, which he greedily swallowed while Mr. Fox looked on. Every time the stork pulled up a frog he invited the fox to do the same. But the fox could only sit on his haunches, staring at the jar, and trying to hide both his annoyance and his hunger. At last the stork finished up all the frogs, and then, for the first time, broke into a croaking laugh.

" Ah ! Mr. Fox ! Mr. Fox ! " said he. " You thought to make fun of my long neck and bill. But I think the laugh is on my side to-night, for I have paid back your practical joke with interest ! "

THE FROGS WHO ASKED FOR A KING

AMONG the reeds on the banks of a great
lake lived the Frog-People, who thought
that the lake was their own property, as
Frog-Country surrounded it on every side. The
frogs were very fond of making laws—they made
one every morning and broke it every night.
Anybody who walked near the lake at dawn or
at twilight would always hear them making a
most terrific croaking. That was when they
were quarrelling at the tops of their voices about
their laws.

At last they decided that, as the more laws
they made the more they broke, they had better
have a King-Frog to keep order. So they sent
ambassadors to Jupiter, who, as I daresay you
know, lived on a mountain and was the King
of the eagles, and of the cuckoos, and of a great
many other creatures as well—and asked him
to send them a ruler. Jupiter listened, laughing
to himself. He thought the Frog-People a set
of foolish fellows, and he determined to play
a joke on them. So he promised the ambassadors

they should have a king ; and, as soon as they had hopped joyfully away, he sent a great log rolling over and over down the mountain side, until, with a tremendous crash, it bowled into the water of the lake.

What a splash it made, to be sure, and how frightened the Frog-People were at the noisy arrival of their new King. They all made one long hop into their holes, and hid there, breathless ; so terrified, indeed, that for three days, at least, they did not make a single new law. Then, as this remarkable King never moved, but just lay where he had fallen, the frogs crept out one by one, and began to approach him timidly.

"Your majesty," they murmured to him, "we are delighted to welcome you, although we were a little overcome at first by the magnificence of your arrival!" But to all their fine speeches, King Log did not make sound or movement in reply.

This went on for some time, and at last the frogs lost all fear of their King. They swam about him, climbed on to his back, and, very likely, played leap-frog over him. Then they decided that he was no good at all as a King, so they sent ambassadors a second time to Jupiter to ask for a better.

Jupiter shrugged his shoulders, laughed again, and sent an Eel into the lake, where it crawled at its ease in the mud, taking no notice of the frogs whatever, and eating most of the worms that they wanted to eat themselves. Whenever the frogs asked King Eel if it approved of their laws it only wriggled a little deeper into the mud, to save itself the trouble of answering. So, quite disgusted with Its Majesty, the frogs sent to Jupiter a third time, saying that King Log and King Eel were both failures and would he not make another effort to please them.

This day Jupiter happened to be a little out of temper. So, instead of laughing at the Frog-People for their silliness, he determined to punish them. That evening a magnificent bird, with wide-spread wings, and legs trailing out behind, came flapping through the air at sunset, making a loud croaking, not unlike the frogs' own, only deeper and hoarser. He alighted among the reeds, and stood there on his long legs, the light shining upon his slender neck and pale grey feathers. His neck was so long and he stood so still that he looked like a tiny signpost pointing out the way to somewhere. He was King Heron, and the frogs set up a chorus of joy, for they felt that at last they really had a King who was worthy of his subjects.

King Heron peered enquiringly into the lake, taking no notice of the Frog-People. He was seeking fish for his supper. But the pretty silver fishes did not like muddy Frog-Country, and none were to be seen. A rather forward young frog swam up to King Heron, kicking its green legs out in the finest swimming-stroke it knew, in order to explain matters. But King Heron— who was very hungry—thought that a frog might be better for supper than nothing; and, putting his long neck down in a wonderful loop, he swallowed the pert young frog in a single mouthful.

So it went on, day after day, and week after week. King Heron used to stand all day—and most of the night—among the sedges, eating the frogs as soon as they came within reach of his long neck and bill. Now and then he waded deeper into the water for more. And at last no frogs at all were left in the Frog-Country, for King Heron had gobbled up every one of them.

So, you see, the frogs would have done a great deal better if they had been sensible enough to make just a few laws and stick to them; then they would never have been made fun of by King Log and King Eel, nor swallowed, in the end, by King Heron.

THE BOYS AND THE FROGS

SOME little boys—let us hope there were no little girls among them—caught sight, one day, of a lot of green frogs hopping cheerfully around a pond.

"There are some frogs!" said they to each other. "Let's throw stones at them!"

So they set to work to throw stones at the frogs, just for the fun of the thing. When they killed one, it seemed to them to be rare sport, and they shouted their successes at the tops of their voices. But, after a time, an old frog put its head out of the water, opened its mouth widely, and spoke.

The small boys were so surprised to hear a frog speak, that they stood quite still, the stones in their hands. And what do you think the old frog said?

Well, you have probably heard the words many and many a time. It said very gravely:

"Boys! Be good enough to stop throwing stones. For what is fun to you is death to us!"

Then it put its head back into the water, and

" 'Boys!' said the frog. 'Be good enough to stop throwing stones. For what is fun to you is death to us!' "

we will hope that all the little boys went home. But the old frog's words, spoken hundreds and hundreds of years ago, have been a proverb ever since.

"What is fun to you is death to us."

It is a proverb that gives people a good deal to think about.

THE MISER

THERE once lived a man who was a terrible miser.

Whenever he got any money he never thought of the pleasant and good things he could do with it, but only of the best way to hide it, so that nobody could steal it from him. He put it in this place and that, thinking first one and then the other the safer. At last he hid all of it in a big hole in the cellar, and placed a heavy stone on the top.

By this time he was so afraid of being robbed that he seldom gave himself even the pleasure of lifting the stone and peeping at the gold below. But one day, when he had not seen his money for several months, he thought he would give himself the treat of counting it over.

He crept down to the cellar in the dark, with a candle to light the way. Very cautiously, he lifted the stone and set it aside. Then he gave a great cry of horror and dismay. There was not so much as a penny piece lying in the hole

" The miser gave a great cry of horror and dismay. There was not so much as a penny piece lying in the hole."

L

—some thief who had found out about the gold had come long ago and stolen it.

The miser moaned his loss so loudly that the neighbours came running to see what was the matter. Pointing to the stone and to the hole, he poured out his story in tones of despair. But one of the neighbours told him he need not be in the least unhappy about what had happened.

" See," said the wise man, " I will put the stone back again over the hole—so! As, for months gone by, you have never done anything but come and look at the stone, you can go on doing the same for months to come! Whether the money is there or not can make no more difference to you in the future than it has made in the past. Just go on staring at the stone and live your life as usual ! "

With this good advice all the other neighbours agreed. So they went away quite cheerfully and left the miser sitting alone in the cellar with the candle and the stone.

THE MERCHANT AND HIS FRIEND

A CERTAIN merchant, who had to leave his native town for a time, thought it would be a wise plan to put somebody in charge of his belongings while he was away. He was not very rich, and he did not want to come home to find himself poorer than when he had set off. His business was to buy and sell iron ; and he happened, at the moment, to have quite a lot of iron bars stored in the attic above his shop.

He went, therefore, to a friend whom he thought an honest and trustworthy man, and begged him to take care of the iron for a few weeks. The friend consented willingly, and the merchant started on his travels contentedly, sure that, on his return, he would find all the iron in the store-room where he had left it.

His journey was not successful, for he lost more money than he had hoped to make, and he would have come home in a sad state of mind if he had not been cheered by the thought that he still owned a lot of iron. But his friend met him with a terribly long face and a still longer story.

"Alas!" said this faithless man, "I am the most unhappy of caretakers. You know the iron bars that you left in my charge?"

"Do I not know them?" replied the merchant. "Have I not counted them over fifty times and added up just how much they were worth? What about them?"

The friend shook his head from side to side and looked more miserable than ever.

"A rat!" he said earnestly. "A rat! It got into the store-room and ate every bit of your iron! Come and see!"

The merchant went up to his empty store-room and looked round. Then he spoke as gravely as a judge:

"Ah, this is indeed sad for both of us. But I know how dearly rats love iron. They would rather eat it any day than the finest of cheeses. Indeed, I have lost hundreds of pounds before now through their determination to devour it. Think no more of the matter, my friend. It is not your fault in any way. It is all the fault of that hungry and iron-loving rat."

The friend agreed, well pleased with himself. Thinking that he had indeed hit upon a splendid story to tell the merchant, he pressed that simple-minded man to come to dinner the following

" 'Last night,' said the merchant, 'I saw an owl carrying a child high into the clouds in his claws. If that child was your son, you are never likely to see him again.' "

L*

evening. The merchant accepted the invitation as politely as it was given, and the friend went cheerfully off to his own home, and ordered a particularly excellent meal.

Meanwhile the merchant took a quiet stroll in the same direction. By and by he met one of his friend's children. Taking the little boy by the hand, he led him to his own house. There he hid him, safely and comfortably, in a little secret room near the roof.

The next day he went to the friend's house for dinner, as if nothing unusual had happened. But he found his host in terrible distress.

" Oh, I have had a sad blow! " he cried, tears running down his cheeks. " One of my dear children is lost and cannot be found anywhere. The town-crier has gone round, telling the story, and begging anyone who knows of his whereabouts to come forward. But of no avail! He has disappeared as completely as if the earth had opened and swallowed him up! "

" Ah! " said the merchant, sitting down to his soup sedately, " this is a sad tale you are telling me. I am afraid you have lost your son for ever, because, do you know, last night I saw an owl carrying a child high into the clouds in his claws. If that child was your son, you are never likely to see him again."

"An owl! " cried the friend, his grief giving

way to indignant surprise. " How can you tell me such a ridiculous story! An owl only weighs a few pounds! How in the world could he carry off a child weighing fifty ? "

But the merchant remained sedate and grave as ever.

" This is a strange country, you see," he observed dryly. " If it contains a rat that can eat over a hundred tons of iron, it is equally likely to hold an owl that can carry a child who weighs fifty pounds! I see no reason then why you, of all men, should not believe my story ! "

Then the friend knew he had been found out, and that the merchant was anything but the foolish fellow he had pretended to be. With proper humility, he confessed his theft, and begged that the merchant would in the same way tell him the truth about his lost child. So the merchant rose from the table, dignified as usual :

" If you will take me to the room in your house where you have hidden my iron," said he, " I will lead you to the chamber in mine where I have hidden your son. And the next time you want to steal simple folk's property you had better ask yourself whether the robber is not sometimes a bigger fool than the robbed."

THE TWO BAGS

DID you know that every little boy—and every little girl also for that matter— has two bags hanging round his neck as he sits at his lessons or runs about at his play?

They are such funny bags that I can't tell you what they are made of, but it is some sort of wonderful fairy stuff. The one that hangs in front is very small, and the one that hangs behind is very big. The little boys—and the little girls —know all about the bags that hang under their chins, but very little about those that dangle between their shoulders. Shall I tell you what the front bags hold?

We will suppose that we know of a little boy called Tommy. Well, Tommy often takes a glance at the bag he wears in front, and he sees that it holds all the faults that are so ugly in other little boys—Ned's bad temper, and Willie's sulks, and Johnnie's fibs, and Harry's conceit. And he feels very grand and superior because there is nothing at all in the bag that belongs to Tommy!

But meanwhile the other bag hangs right

behind his back, where he cannot look into it at all. What do you think he would see if he could ? He would see Tommy's bad temper, and Tommy's sulks, and Tommy's fibs, and Tommy's conceit, all jostling each other in a bag that, although it is so big, will hardly hold them.

What a pity it is that he does not sometimes manage to change the places of the two bags, and then he would find out how very big Tommy's faults are and how very small those of Willie, and Johnnie, and Harry and Ned !

THE WOLF AND THE FOX

ONE summer evening a big red fox—who, as you will know quite well after all the stories you have read about foxes, belongs to the slyest company of rogues in the world—set out on his nightly ramble through the fields, looking for supper. The moon was shining overhead, but, as he kept his eyes fixed on the little wavings among the shadowy grass, he did not see the crystal ball that hung high above. By and by he came to a low, round wall, built of stones, with a stone arch above it, with a sort of pulley set atop. From the pulley hung two ropes, and each rope had a bucket tied to the end of it. One bucket was low down; the other high up near the arch.

Full of curiosity, the fox stood up on his hind legs, and set his paws on the little low wall. Then he saw that he was looking into a deep well with water at the bottom. And, in the very middle of the water, shone the round reflection of the moon!

"Oh, oh!" said the fox to himself, "I am in

luck ! Never have I seen such a remarkably fine cheese ! ”

He licked his lips, and leant a little further over the low wall, quite sure that the reflection of the moon was a cheese ! Then he set his wits to work, thinking over a hundred plans by which he might reach the cheese and eat it for his supper.

As he sat thinking, a girl hurried round the corner with a pitcher. She had come from a little house with lights in the windows, on the edge of the forest. Instantly Mr. Fox hid himself in the brushwood. But he kept his cunning eyes wide open to see what she would do.

What she did was to pull the bucket that was at the bottom of the well up to the top of the little wall. The other bucket went down as its fellow came up full of water. The girl filled her pitcher with the water, and hurried home in the moonlight as fast as she had come.

“ Ha ! ” said Mr. Fox to himself, slipping like a red shadow from the brushwood. “ Now I see the way to get at the cheese in the bottom of the well ! ”

Into the bucket he sprang, as it hung, dangling, at the end of the rope. Down it went with the weight of him, and up came the other bucket from the bottom. Mr. Fox sat in his strange carriage, his head thrust eagerly over the rim.

THE WOLF AND THE FOX

But when he reached the water he found that he had been sadly mistaken in his idea that this bright object (the reflection of the moon, as it proved) was a cheese!

What a foolish fellow he must have felt, sitting supperless, in a dangling bucket at the bottom of the well! But he said to himself hopefully:

" Soon the girl will come again with the pitcher. She will send the other bucket down and this bucket will go up! Then I can jump out and find something else for supper, as what I thought was a cheese is only the reflection of the moon in the water! "

But the night passed, and the girl did not come. Then the morning broke, and a whole day sent its changing lights and shadows through the wood. Evening fell again. And unhappy Mr. Fox still sat in the bucket at the bottom of the well.

The moon rose, and he felt dreadfully annoyed with it for having persuaded him that its reflection was a cheese. Then, all at once, a great shadowy head appeared between the moonlight and the round hole at the top of the well. A wolf was looking down at him, asking what in the world he was doing in the bucket!

This was Mr. Fox's opportunity. Hungry as he was, he made his voice very strong and gracious.

" What am I doing ? " said he. " I am eating the most delicious cheese you ever tasted ! "

" Cheese ? " replied the wolf. " Where ? "

" Here, at the bottom of the well, to be sure ! Wouldn't you like some ? "

" Very much indeed, thank you, Mr. Fox. But how can I get down ? "

" In the other bucket, of course ! That was the way I came ! "

Into the bucket at the top hopped Mr. Wolf, mightily pleased at the thought of the cheese. As his bucket went down, Mr. Fox's bucket came up. They passed each other on the way, and it is difficult to say which was the more delighted —Mr. Wolf at the thought of getting into the well, or Mr. Fox at the thought of getting out of it !

The Fox reached the top, and sprang gladly on to the firm green grass. From the bottom came a howl from Mr. Wolf.

" Where is the cheese ? Hi ! Stop ! Answer ! Where is the cheese ? "

Mr. Fox put his head for a moment over the little stone wall that was built about the well.

" When you have found it you can eat it," was all he said. " For my part I have had enough ! "

And off he galloped to look for rabbits, while

" But when the fox reached the water he found
that he had been sadly mistaken in his idea
that this bright object (the reflection of the
moon, as it proved) was a cheese ! "

poor Mr. Wolf howled dismally after him. Whether he found out that the cheese was only the reflection of the moon, or whether he ever managed to get out of the well again, the story does not tell. But it shows that Mr. Fox had managed to learn a thing or two about buckets, and pulleys, and the best way to save his own skin in a difficulty.

THE MONKEY AND THE CHEESE

TWO cats, a tabby and a black-and-white, once helped each other to steal a large piece of cheese from the kitchen cupboard, and carried it out into a quiet corner of the garden to eat. When they reached a nice hidden spot behind some bushes they set down the cheese and licked their lips delightedly.

"What a large piece we have managed to get," said Mrs. Tabby. "It must measure quite four inches across!"

"Four inches!" replied Miss Black-and-White, with a snort of contempt. "It's five inches if it's the length of my shortest claw!"

Mrs. Tabby did not like being contradicted by a mere spinster. She glared out of her green eyes and said firmly:

"A married cat, who has brought up at least seven families, cannot be mistaken about the size of a piece of cheese. I say it is four inches, and that's all!"

"*Five* inches!" snarled Miss Black-and-White. "I declare it's five!"

THE MONKEY AND THE CHEESE

Mrs. Tabby was just going to spit out " *Four*," when Mr. Monkey came round the corner of the bushes. He lived in the same house as the cats, and was quite friendly with them.

" Pray, ladies, what is the matter ? " said he.

Both cats began talking at once, explaining that they were arguing about the size of the piece of cheese, and asked him to decide. Mr. Monkey looked at the cheese, grave as a judge. Then he took it into his paws.

" It is difficult to determine," said he. " For one thing, the piece is such an odd shape ! If I were to bite out a bit at this side, now——"

He put the cheese to his mouth and took a large bite out of it. Then he held it solemnly towards the cats.

" It is quite a nice shape now, and much easier to judge," said he. " What is your present opinion on the matter ? "

Both cats gazed earnestly at the piece of cheese. They were thinking much more, now, of their quarrel than of how good the cheese would be to eat.

" Three and a half inches ! " declared Mrs. Tabby—and was instantly contradicted by Miss Black-and-White.

" Four and a half," hissed the spinster cat. " Mrs. Tabby has not the slightest idea of size ! "

" Well she might *mi-au*, for Mr. Monkey had
put the whole bit of cheese into his mouth!"

" Dear me ! Dear me ! " said the monkey. " We shall have to try again ! "

Once more he set his teeth in the cheese. This time he took a much larger mouthful, and held out the piece that was left for the cats to look at.

" Well ? " he said, still very gravely. " Surely you can agree upon the matter this time ! "

" Two inches ! " cried Mrs. Tabby. But before the words were out of her mouth Miss Black-and-White had interrupted her.

" Three ! " rapped out Miss Black-and-White. " No less than three ! "

" Ah ! " murmured Mr. Monkey thoughtfully.

Again he gazed at the cheese with an innocent expression. Then he bit a third time, and, once more, displayed what was left to the cats.

" One inch ! " snapped Mrs. Tabby, all the fur on her back standing on end. " I vow it's only one ! "

" And *I* vow it's one and three-quarters," Miss Black-and-White squealed at the top of her voice, ending up with a *mi-au* that you might have heard from one end of the garden to the other. Well she might *mi-au*, for Mr. Monkey had put the whole bit of cheese into his mouth and swallowed it !

" I have done my best to help you, ladies," said he, "but my efforts have been quite useless. I wish you both a very good afternoon ! "

THE WIDOW AND HER LITTLE MAIDENS

IN a pretty little cottage once lived a tidy old widow, who wore the cleanest caps and the finest kerchiefs you ever saw in your life. She was, oh, so fond of washing and scrubbing and baking and sewing! Everybody who knew her used to say that she was the hardest working body they had ever seen, and an example to the whole neighbourhood.

This good woman had two little girls living with her, whom she was always trying to make as clean and tidy as herself. She taught them how to knead bread, and to bake pies, and to spin fine thread on their spinning-wheels. Every morning, the moment the big brown cock in the yard gave his first crow, she would get out of bed, go to the room where the little girls slept, and shake them until they woke.

"Get up! Get up!" she would say. "Don't you hear the cock crowing outside? The sun will be shining over the hill in a moment. Nobody in this house must stay in bed when once the cock has crowed!"

" ' Get up ! Get up ! ' the woman would say.
' Don't you hear the cock crowing outside ? ' "

M*

THE WIDOW AND HER LITTLE MAIDENS

The little girls were always dreadfully sleepy, and did not want to get up in the least. But the bustling old woman would stand over them till they got out of bed, yawning and blinking their eyes. Then she would trot off to her household work, telling them to wash and dress and to follow her into the kitchen as quickly as they could.

Now one of the things the little girls had to do was to feed the poultry—the big brown cock among the others. He was rather a greedy cock, and always ate a lot of the scraps and corn that were thrown on to the ground. The old lady would stand at the kitchen door to watch the feeding, and the more the cock ate the better she was pleased.

" Is he not a fine fellow ? " she would say to the little girls. " Be sure and give him the best tit-bits. If it were not for him we should always be oversleeping ourselves, for there would be nobody to wake us in the morning ! "

Then the little girls would look at each other under their eyelashes and pout. For both of them hated the cock ! They thought he was a very tiresome bird to wake everybody at sunrise, when it would be so much nicer to sleep on until eight or nine o'clock.

At last, one day, when the cock seemed to have crowed even earlier than usual, they decided they could stand it no longer. They waited until their mistress had gone to market, then they caught the poor brown cock and wrung his neck! After which they buried him, as quickly as they could, in the field on the other side of the fence. Then, rather frightened at what they had done, they set to work to bake the cakes for supper.

The old lady came home by and by, and, of course, she soon missed the cock. High and low she hunted for him, while the little girls kept as much out of her way as possible. When they went to bed, however, they told each other how glad they were that they had killed the horrid cock at last.

"Now," they said to each other, "we shall have a little peace. How lovely it will be to sleep as long as we want to, with no cock crowing to wake our mistress in the morning!"

They cuddled down into their pillows and fell asleep. But in the middle of the night—or so it seemed to them—the old lady trotted to their bedside in her night-cap, carrying a lighted candle!

"Get up! Get up!" she said to them, all in a bustle. "We have no cock to wake us now, and it will never do to oversleep ourselves! The dawn has not broken yet, I know! But it will break presently, and without the crowing in the yard we shall not even know that day has come. Get up! Get up! Follow me into the kitchen as quickly as possible!"

How cross and disappointed those little maidens were! But they were obliged to do as their mistress told them. So up they got, and started baking and scrubbing, and washing, and spinning by candle-light, sleepier than they had ever been in their lives.

And as the old lady had been too fond of the cock to wish to buy another to take his place, she went on waking up the little girls in the middle of the night, insisting on them getting up to work, lest a single minute of the coming daylight should be wasted.

Oh, how those two blinking, yawning, little girls wished that they had never killed the big brown cock!

THE LIONESS'S SON

ONCE upon a time there was a tremendous fuss and quarrelling among all the animals. They were arguing hotly about which had the finest children! Every one of them, from the frogs and the caterpillars to the rabbits and the rats, declared that no families had ever been born like *their* families, and that it was a great pity their children, and grandchildren, and great-grandchildren were not numerous enough to fill the whole world. Anyway, they said, they would go on doing their best. The caterpillars and frogs would lay eggs by the hundred; the rabbits would make new warrens; and the rats would take possession of ever so many more drains. Then, surely, it would be agreed that a caterpillar, or a frog, a rat, or a rabbit, had the honour of giving to the world the finest children that had ever been born in it.

They were all agreed upon one thing, in spite of the quarrelling. This was that they would wait just one year, and then go to King Jupiter on his mountain, and ask him to settle the matter for them. So, for a year, they laid their dispute aside. At the end of it, they sent a message to the King of the mountain saying that they would do themselves the honour of calling upon him, and would bring all their families along with them.

King Jupiter sat on his shining throne, and up the sides of the mountain came the long strings of animals. Mount Olympus had seen some strange sights, but perhaps this procession was the oddest of all. First came a Father and Mother Hedgehog. Very squat they were—very brown and prickly. They were followed by seven little hedgehogs, just as prickly, just as brown, and just as squat. When they saw King Jupiter they were all so startled that they rolled themselves up into balls, and lay quite still in front of him. But, even in this rather ridiculous position, Mother Hedgehog might be heard murmuring, from the middle of her stiffened spines, many things about the beauty and number of her children.

The hedgehogs had to make way, however, for a much larger party—a whole family of lizards. As well as Mr. and Mrs. Lizard, there were twelve little misses and masters of the same name. They were smooth, yellowish little creatures, with quick legs, and tails that flicked about like whips. They darted all over the top of the mountain, catching flies, and no doubt amused King Jupiter very much. But they, too, had to move aside to allow him to pass judgment upon a colony of frogs.

If numbers were to win the prize of excellence, surely the frogs had it ! The father and mother, solemn, goggle-eyed and fat, were followed by at least a hundred hop-o'-my-thumbs just like themselves, though ever so much smaller. They had all come straight out of a shallow pond in a heavy shower that very morning, scrambling through the wet grass, and hopping along the turnpike road, so that the country folks thought they had fallen out of the clouds together with the rain. But they hadn't done any such thing ! They were only skipping along after their father and mother to hear what King Jupiter had to say about them.

So it went on all through that strange and wonderful day on Mount Olympus. The caterpillars came ; the rats came ; the rabbits came. And all of them brought a regular tribe of children, none of them a year old. Then up trotted the foxes, and the badgers, the weasels, and the stoats, each with four or five youngsters apiece. But at last, up the hill path, came a lioness, beautiful and strong. And she had only one child, a little creature with golden eyes, and splendid limbs. She led him up to Jupiter, and, sitting on her haunches, surveyed her glorious child in silence.

Then King Jupiter came down from his bright throne, and holding up his sceptre, gave his decision in a clear and ringing voice.

" Listen, you fathers and mothers of rabbits, hedgehogs and frogs ! It is true that you have all produced a great many children in the past year, and that the lioness has only produced one. But that one is a *lion* ! To the lioness, therefore, I give the prize. Her child shall, from now, be called Royal. I name him, from to-day, the King of all the beasts."

He touched the little lion's head for a moment with his sceptre. Then the lioness turned away, still in silence, and led her son back to her cave at the foot of the mountain. She had taken no part in the boasting of the lesser animals, yet she had always known that her son was the finest creature ever given to the world. She had only one child—but, as Jupiter had said, that only child was a lion.

THE MILKMAID AND HER PAIL

ALL along a flowery meadow tripped the prettiest milkmaid in the world, carrying her pail upon her head as cleverly as possible. Her name was Perette, and she had pink cheeks and blue eyes and golden curls; and well she knew that the farm-lads and shepherds all peeped admiringly through the hedge at her as she passed. But she pretended not to see them, for she was filled with a wonderful dream.

"This milk is worth a lot of money!" thought she. "I will take it to the town and sell it, and then I can buy at least four sittings of eggs. I will bring the eggs home, and put them under four of my best and biggest and brownest hens. In three weeks time each hen will bring out thirteen chicks, and I shall have fifty-two of the pretty little yellow things to feed. I can rear them on scraps until the autumn, and then I will run them on the barley-stubble, which will cost nothing at all! By Christmas there will be fifty-two big beautiful fowls for sale! Oh! what a lot of money I shall have!"

" When Perette tossed her head she tossed the
pail with it, and all the fresh white milk fell
down into the buttercups and lay there in
a big pool, with the empty pail alongside."

THE MILKMAID AND HER PAIL

She clapped her little hands softly together, and almost danced along through the buttercups; though she had to dance very carefully on account of the milk.

"With the money I will go to the best shop in the town and buy my dress for the Christmas parties. It shall be blue satin trimmed with lace! I will have pink silk stockings and silver shoes, a long chain of beads, and a fan, and a wreath of red roses fastened at each side of my head with a pearl comb! Then all the boys (who are staring at me now through the hedge) will come and say, 'Oh! Perette, you sweet pretty girl, won't you give me a dance?' And I shall toss my head—so—and answer proudly——"

But what Perette's proud answer would have been nobody will ever know; for by now she had quite forgotten the milk. So, when she tossed her head, she tossed the pail with it, and all the fresh white milk fell down into the buttercups and lay there in a big pool, with the empty pail alongside. Then Perette sat down in the hedge and cried with disappointment.

"How foolish I have been!" sobbed she. "If I had not counted my chickens before they were hatched I should never have thought about tossing my head at the party, and so should never have thrown down my pail of milk!"

THE DRAGON IN THE MOON

AN astronomer once built a high tower, set up a tall telescope in it, and spent all his nights staring through the telescope at the sky.

He saw wonderful things through that round piece of glass; stars bright as fireflies and big as roses made in gold; a moon all wide and wonderful, with still mountains, like shadows, pushing up into its silver spaces; and sometimes blazing comets that swept the high distances with the shining splendour of their tails.

At last he got so moon-struck that he forgot all about the things that happen in the day-light, and thought only of the marvels of the night.

Everything he saw in the dark seemed to him more wonderful than the last. So he was not surprised when, one evening, on putting his eager eye to the telescope, he saw a dragon sitting in the very middle of the moon!

It had a strange body, blue and shining, as if made of a sapphire-stone; big wings like stained

" The astronomer ran round the town knocking
up all his friends from their beds. 'Come
and see! Come and see!' he called up to
their windows. 'I have found out that a
dragon lives in the moon.'"

windows, clear, yet tinged with purple and green ; ever so many legs, hairy and long ; and eyes that were a perfect marvel of brightness, set in its big cunning head. It remained perfectly still, as if the moon was a cave and it was a great and mysterious monster asleep in the middle of it.

The astronomer was so excited he hardly knew what to do. For a long time he stared at the entrancing picture ; then he hurried down the stairs of the tower, and ran round the town, knocking up all his friends from their beds.

" Come and see ! Come and see ! " he called up to their windows. " I have made the greatest discovery ever made in the history of science. I have found out that a dragon lives in the moon."

The affair was so exciting that most of his friends got up, and, dressing as quickly as possible, hurried to the tower. Soon quite a crowd of people were gathered on the roof, waiting their turn to look through the telescope. And each one, as he looked, exclaimed aloud about the blue body, the shining glassy wings, the hairy legs, and the brilliant eyes, of the dragon that was stretched out, fast asleep, in the middle of the moon.

At last an old, grave, very clever astronomer came up to the telescope, and set his eyes to the glass. He looked, and looked, listening to the exclamations all about him, with the oddest little smile. Then, quite quietly, he unscrewed the end of the telescope and took off the cap. And there, fast stuck against the glass, was a small fly!

"My friend," said the old astronomer to the young one, "your discovery was very marvellous! But sometimes it is wiser to look into your own telescope for the reason why it shows you the picture of a dragon in the moon!"

THE HERMIT AND THE MOUSE

IN a beautiful and quiet forest dwelt a hermit. He had lived there so long that he understood the language of all the birds and beasts. One day he was seated at the door of his cave, when, down from the clouds, as it seemed, there fell a tiny mouse. The moment the little creature saw the hermit, it ran into his long white beard for safety, and hid under the good man's chin.

" Where did you come from, my little friend ? " asked the hermit in astonishment.

" Oh, save me ! save me ! " squeaked the mouse. " I fell out of the beak of a great cruel hawk, who was carrying me to her nest for her babies' supper ! "

Now the hermit had vowed to protect all small and weak things, so he put the little mouse into a safe corner of the cave, and gave it a meal of rice. The hawk, meanwhile, flew far away and found something else for her children to eat that evening.

The mouse, so kindly cared for by the hermit, grew sleek and fat. And, then, one fine after-

" The mouse was immediately turned into a lady-cat, with a tortoise-shell coat."

noon, what should come walking along the woodland path but a great tom-cat?

The mouse peeped at the cat in terror, and the cat sat down in the sunshine and licked his near hind-leg in the wonderful way cats have. The mouse was more alarmed than ever when it saw its enemy's white teeth and long pink tongue. It went to the very farthest corner of the cave and squeaked pitifully.

" What is the matter now? " asked the hermit, kind as usual.

" Oh, good sir! good sir! " replied the mouse, " I am frightened to death by that big tom-cat! "

" Oh, that is easily set right! " replied the hermit. And he waved his hands over the mouse, which was immediately turned into a lady-cat, with a tortoise-shell coat, and eyes of the most attractive shade of green. With great pride, this lovely creature now walked out of the cave, and, sitting down within a yard of the tom-cat, mewed at him languidly!

The two cats were soon great friends; but, one evening, as they sat nose to nose, the tom-cat suddenly gave a squeak of fright, and its fur stood up like a chimney-sweep's brush. With a bound it disappeared into the trees, as, round the corner, came an enormous dog! The hermit's cat fled into the cave again, and once more her kind master asked what was the matter.

" Oh, that dog ! " shuddered the cat. " That horrible, hungry dog ! "

" Dear me, I cannot allow you to be frightened by a dog ! " declared the hermit. Waving his hands again, he changed his cat into a dog much larger than the new-comer, who, when he saw what a fierce creature lived inside the hermit's cave, turned tail and hurriedly trotted away.

So now the hermit had a dog for a companion, and the dog kept the good man busy supplying him with food. But, one morning, the dog awakened his master from his sleep with howls of anguish.

" Oh, the tiger ! " wailed the dog. " There is an awful tiger sitting in the bushes over yonder ! I know quite well that, if I put so much as the tip of my nose out of the cave, he will make his breakfast off me ! Oh, kind master, do something to protect me from the tiger ! "

" You shall protect yourself ! " declared the hermit. And he made all haste with his magic, and turned his dog into a second tiger, who immediately drove the first tiger off.

So now the hermit lived quite a pleasant and leisurely life with a tiger ! The good man was not in the least disturbed by his strange companion, of whom, in his heart, he never thought of but as a mouse ! However, the story got abroad, and people from the villages beyond the forest began to visit the hermit to see the tiger who had gone through so many wonderful transformations.

The tiger, blinking in the sunshine, heard these people whispering to one another as they peeped at him from a safe distance.

" See that tiger ! Doesn't he look fierce and big and strong ? Who would believe that the hermit could make such a marvellous beast out of a little miserable mouse ? "

The handsome tiger, hearing this said over and over again, grew very annoyed " What is all this ? What is all this ? " he growled. " Am I, a lordly tiger, to be continually reminded that I was once a mouse ? I will see to it that everybody knows I am a tiger in earnest, and that the story of my early days is forgotten ! " With which he brandished his tail, licked his lips, and set off in search of his master, to eat him up !

But the hermit saw him coming, and, because he was such a great wizard, read what was in the ungrateful animal's mind. Hey, presto ! he just laughed and waved his hand about the tiger's head before the cruel creature had time to leap upon him. In the twinkling of an eye the tiger dwindled into something so tiny that he almost disappeared. He tried to roar, but he could only give the very smallest squeak. His master had turned him back into a mouse!

What became of the mouse in the end this old, old Indian story does not tell us. There is no doubt the ungrateful little thing thoroughly deserved to be eaten by the hawk's children. But who, after all, could expect anything really lordly and noble from a tiger who had begun life as a mouse?

THE TIGER'S GOLDEN BRACELET

THIS is a story of something that must certainly have happened long ago in India, for there cannot be another country where so strange a thing could take place.

It happened on a long white road, down which many travellers used to pass, some of them going to the north and some to the south. By the side of the road ran a great river, with wide marshy banks overgrown with tall reeds. And, one fine morning, the travellers who went down the road saw a big old tiger seated on the far bank of the river, looking out over the water at everybody who went by.

The glossy striped beast kept very still, but as the travellers, mounted either on camels or on donkeys, came within hearing, they were all astonished to hear the tiger calling to them. His strange voice travelled across the stream, clear and ringing as a hollow brass bell.

"Ho! Ho! Traveller! Take this golden bracelet!"

Those were the strange words that echoed.

from bank to bank of the river. As the tiger
called, he waved a big bunch of grasses in his
paw. This he did to show that he was an extremely good tiger, who would never do harm to
anybody; for the grasses were of a kind only
gathered by priests and other holy men.

Well, the travellers heard the tiger calling—
and very much amazed they were. But, though
all of them stood still to listen, nobody was
silly enough to step through the reeds into the
river, to say nothing of meeting the tiger face
to face on the other side. So they shook their
heads and rode on, while the tiger continued to
wave his bunch of grasses, and to call out to
the next person who approached—

"Ho! Ho! Traveller! Take this golden
bracelet."

This went on all day, and at last evening
fell, and the tiger had found nobody who would
take the golden bracelet. Then a man came
quite alone down the road in the twilight, and
the tiger's call rang, once more, across the water,
very loud and clear.

"Ho! Ho! Traveller! Take this golden
bracelet!"

The man started. Looking over the river, he
saw the big tiger seated among the reeds on
the opposite side. So down went the traveller
to the edge of the water that he might stare more

closely at this strange beast who was offering him a golden bracelet. When he got there, however, he stopped short, afraid to go further. And there he began to argue with himself.

" It is not wise," said the traveller aloud, " to step down into strange rivers ! Sometimes they have deep holes in them ! It is certainly still less wise to trust animals with claws or horns ! Sometimes they scratch, or toss you ! In order to get the golden bracelet I must trust both the river and the tiger ! And I have *heard* that tigers, now and then, eat people up. And this is a matter on which the opinion of other folk deserves serious consideration ! "

He was really quite a sensible traveller, you see, and, if he had followed his own reasoning he would have hurried off through the reeds again, stepped back on to the road, and continued his journey. But, though he argued well, the tiger, who was a very clever fellow, set to work to argue better.

" How uncharitable," said the tiger, " to think such things of a poor harmless beast who is merely offering you a golden bracelet ! If you wanted to give a beautiful present to a tiger, would you consider it kind of the tiger to declare you were only coaxing him into a trap ? Why not judge me by yourself ? "

The traveller humm'd and ha'd, and at last

asked where the tiger kept the golden bracelet. The tiger held up a paw high above the rushes, and there was the bracelet gleaming on what stood for his wrist. "It is a real golden bracelet!" cried the big beast, very earnestly. "I can assure you of that! See how it shines when I twist it about!"

Still the traveller hesitated, and asked the tiger how he could trust him. The tiger shook his head, and blinked his eyes with a saintly look.

"In my youth," said he, "I was a very wicked tiger and ate up ever so many men and a still greater number of cows! I was punished by the death of my wife and all my children! So I was advised, by a good hermit, to take to good deeds! I have taken to them in very earnest, and, as a proof of my penitence, I am offering you this golden bracelet from off my own wrist."

The tiger looked so saintly as he spoke, and allowed such large tears of remorse to roll down his striped cheeks, that the traveller was thoroughly taken in at last. He put first one foot, and then the other, into the river, and began to wade across. But the river was no more to be trusted than the tiger! Under the water was a deep mud-bank, in which the traveller immediately stuck fast.

"I will come and help you out!" purred the

"'Oh!' cried the traveller, 'my end has come! This is the result of trusting an animal with claws!'"

tiger softly, and started creeping across the mud-bank in the twilight, waving his great tail. But, when he reached the traveller, instead of pulling him out of the mud, he stood there, licking his lips, and grinning with delight as he prepared to eat the poor man up for supper!

"Oh!" cried the traveller, "my end has come! This is the result of trusting an animal with claws! I might have known that never yet was a tiger born who, in his old age, turned into a saint!"

So the traveller was gobbled up, but a blue pigeon called "Light-Flier" had been sitting on a bough near at hand, and had seen and heard all that happened. And he went about telling the story, the moral of which is that, however much you may be tempted, you should never trust a big old tiger who waves a bunch of grass on a river bank, and offers you a golden bracelet out of his great strong paw.

THE FOX WHO HAD LOST HIS TAIL

EARLY one morning a fine and handsome fox, who had been hunting all night, was slipping home through a gorse covert when—*bing! bang! snap!* a hidden trap caught him by his brush, which he was allowing to hang carelessly behind him. Mr. Fox gave a loud bark of rage and terror, struggled and fought violently, and at last managed to get free. But alas! he had left his beautiful brush in the trap; and he sat down and bewailed the loss, not altogether on account of the pain, but because he felt sure all the other foxes would think him such a poor sort of fellow, going about the world without a tail.

At last, as he sat staring at the brush in the trap, a brilliant idea occurred to him. He blinked his eyes, nodded his head, stood up, and trotted off.

When he reached the earth where he lived he spent a long time licking himself clean and tidy after his accident. Then he sent out invitations to all the other foxes who lived in all the other earths in the neighbourhood. He said, in the invitation, that he had something very interesting and important to tell them.

Well, all the foxes came together and sat in a ring, on their haunches, round the fox who had lost his brush. And Mr. Brushless Fox began to lecture them at great length on the extreme inconvenience, and ugliness, and weight, and trouble of their highly unnecessary tails.

" Of what use is this heavy ugly brush that Nature has seen fit to bestow upon us ? " said he. " Never was there anything so absurd ! We do not wag our tails, as those horrid white and tan creatures, the hounds, do. Nor do we use them, like horses, to whisk away flies, since flies do not buzz below ground with any energy to speak of. As far as I can see, a fox's brush is merely attached to his body so that it can be cut off when he has been hunted to death, and given to some greedy human being to carry home. What a fate ! What an indignity ! In order, then, to improve your appearance while you are alive, and to save your pride when you are dead, I advise you all—*all*—to cut off your tails without further delay."

The foxes listened to him gravely, their bright cunning eyes wide open, their little sharp-nosed heads on one side. He was a crafty old fellow, this brushless fox—but his fellows were even

" He was a crafty old fellow, this brushless fox."

craftier. One of them slipped behind the lecturer and had a good look at his back. Then, coming out into the open, the peeping fox announced his discovery.

" Oh, all ye foxes who sit round," said he. " I have something to say to you ! This fox who is advising you to get rid of your tails is only doing so because he has lost his own ! It is for *that* he insists on the weight and ugliness and inconvenience of a brush ! A pretty story, truly. Go behind him, as I have done, and see his ridiculous appearance for yourselves ! "

So all the other foxes ran round Mr. Brushless Fox, and looked at the place where his tail had been and now was not. And then, in a chorus, they repeated the words of the fox who had found the sly one out.

" Aha ! Aha ! " barked all the foxes mockingly. " You are a clever fellow, aren't you ? But we see through you ! You only want us to cut off our tails because you have lost your own ! "

THE LION IN LOVE

AMONG the thick bushes of a deep wood lived a lion who had been a bachelor all his life. He was a magnificent-looking creature, and had never yet found a lioness he considered good enough for him. He used to toss his tawny mane in the sunshine, and wonder where he could discover the lady with hair that was half so fine. Then, one day, he came across her, in the shape of a girl with long golden curls.

The girl was the daughter of the woodman who lived in a clearing of the forest. When she saw the lion come from the bushes, making large eyes at her, she was frightened out of her wits, and ran home as fast as her legs would carry her. But the lion ran quite as quickly, and arrived at the house just as she was closing and bolting the door.

The big beast sat down in front of the cottage, lifted one great paw, and knocked as loudly as he could. While the sound thudded on the door panels the woodman came into the kitchen from the back. Immediately he went to the door

' The big beast lifted one great paw, and knocked
as loudly as he could."

O*

to open it, but his daughter pulled him away.

"Oh, don't open the door," she cried. "A great lion is there. He followed me home through the forest!"

"What does he want?" enquired the woodman, amazed.

"I don't know," replied his golden-haired daughter, "I only know he looked at me in a way that frightened me out of my wits."

"Tut! Tut!" said the woodman. And he double-locked the door, and put his head carefully out of the window.

There sat the lion, looking not at all fierce, but as sheepish as any country lad who goes courting a pretty girl. He hung his head on one side, and passed his big tongue over his hairy lips.

"Sir," said the lion, with all the dignity he could summon, "I have come to ask for your daughter in marriage."

At this the pretty damsel, who was peeping over her father's shoulder, burst into tears of horror, imploring her father to drive the lion away immediately. This, however, seemed to the woodman to be more easily said than done.

He coughed a little, and cast about in his mind for an excuse. At last he said quite politely:

"But, good Mr. Lion, you are not—are not

quite the sort of fellow that a pretty girl would fall in love with, are you? "

"Why not?" demanded the Lion. "I have a fine golden mane to match your daughter's golden hair."

The woodman heard a still louder sob from his daughter behind him. He hurried to reply:

"Your mane is all that could be desired, Mr. Lion, but what about your great teeth?"

The lion did not answer. He could not deny that his teeth were rather bigger than the pretty little pearly things that showed when the woodman's daughter smiled.

"And your claws!" continued the woodman, seeing his advantage. "My daughter could not possibly live with a husband with such long nails!"

The lion looked down his nails thoughtfully. Certainly they were rather long, he thought to himself. But the cunning woodman seemed to hit upon an idea.

"If, good sir, you would allow me to pull out all your teeth, and to cut off all your claws, I have no doubt, Mr. Lion, that my daughter might be persuaded to consider your proposal. Otherwise, I fear there is no chance for you!"

The lion hesitated, grunted, and seemed inclined to be annoyed. But he caught a glimpse of his lady's beautiful golden hair behind her father's shoulder, and the sight made his eyes glisten with admiration.

"Very well," said he, "you may pull out all my teeth and cut off all my claws, and then, I have no doubt, your daughter will consent to marry me."

So out of the cottage came the woodman, a large pair of scissors in one hand, and a still larger pair of pincers in the other. And he pulled out all the lion's teeth, and cut off all his claws, while his daughter looked on through the keyhole.

"Now," said poor Mr. Lion, rubbing his jaws rather ruefully, but as foolishly in love as ever, "call out your daughter that I may embrace her!"

"Not so!" cried the cunning woodman triumphantly. "Do you think that I am going to give my pretty, sweet daughter to a lion? Why, if she annoyed you, or you got tired of her, you would swallow her whole! Off with you, Mr. Lion, to your cave, and find a wife among your own people, leaving my daughter to find a husband among hers!"

And he took a great club and drove Mr. Lion away from the cottage, for he was not a bit afraid of him now that he had cut off all the big creature's great claws and pulled out all his long and enormous teeth.

THE FLIES IN THE HONEY

A JAR of delicious honey stood in the larder of a cottage ; while, outside the window, the bees who had made the honey hummed cheerily between the sunflowers and the pretty straw hives. Round about the mouth of the jar buzzed the flies. How good the honey looked and smelt, they thought, and how nice it would be to get inside the jar and eat it all up !

Then, one day, a wonderful thing happened for the flies. Somebody knocked the jar over ! As it lay broken on the ground, all the fragrant honey streamed out in a river of gold.

"*Buzz ! buzz ! buzz !*" went the flies. "Now at last we can get at the honey made by those foolish bees, who only store it in combs when, if they liked, they might eat it all up ! "

Down on to the spilt honey flew those greedy little flies, and right in the middle of the sweet and sticky lake they settled. They stuffed and stuffed and stuffed themselves with the delicious food, buzzing their delight to each other in the short intervals of eating. At last all the honey was gobbled up, and the flies bethought themselves of going home to bed.

But, when they tried to fly away, not one of them could stir a foot or lift a wing! The honey was all over them, and they were as helpless as if covered with glue.

They struggled and buzzed, and buzzed and struggled, but nothing was of any use. They were stifled and soaked with honey, and could not look forward to any escape. As they died, one by one, the bees went on contentedly humming and working outside. In the end, one fly buzzed out his last words to his companions:

" The bees are not so foolish as we thought, brothers! They evidently know that, while a little is right enough, one can have too much of a good thing! "

JUPITER AND THE HORSE

HIGH on Mount Olympus, as you all know, lived great Jupiter, the Magician-King, who could do wonderful things whenever he wanted. All sorts of beasts and birds would go to Jupiter to ask favours; and sometimes shepherds and shepherdesses found their way to his shining palace to beg for help. One day, up the mysterious sides of the mountain, trotting steadily through the magic pine trees and crushing the fields of asphodel with his hooves, came a big brown horse!

He walked through the golden doors of the palace, and drew near to King Jupiter as he sat on his magnificent throne. Then he made an altogether surprising request.

"Your Majesty," said the horse, "I have come to beg a great favour from you! It is that you would improve my shape!"

"Improve your shape?" echoed King Jupiter in amazement. "But are you not already the most beautiful animal in creation?"

"No, indeed!" cried the horse, earnestly.

286

JUPITER AND THE HORSE

" I have been thinking the matter over, and I can see a dozen ways in which you could make me handsomer and more impressive than I am."

Jupiter shook his royal head, but prepared himself to listen with due attention to the horse's schemes for his own improvement.

" Well, sire," went on this modest, if mistaken, quadruped, " to begin with, look at my neck! It is a stumpy affair at best! What I should like to see set on my shoulders would be a neck as long and graceful as the neck of a swan!"

" *Neck of a swan!* " murmured Jupiter. " Where in the world—but go on, go on! What next ? "

" My legs ! " replied the horse promptly. " My legs next, your Majesty. They, too, might be a great deal longer, to match my new neck. If they were twice as long, I could gallop twice as fast."

" Possibly—possibly ! " agreed Jupiter in a very half-hearted manner. " And then——"

" Then my chest ! " broke in the horse. " I would like it to be twice as broad, so that I could breathe more deeply. And, since I am tired of being fitted with that most uncomfortable thing, a saddle, I would like a hump made on my back, on which men could seat themselves without girthing me up until I am ready to burst my ribs to get rid of the tightness about them ! "

JUPITER AND THE HORSE

" *Hum! Hum!* " said King Jupiter. " And what do you think you would look like at the end of all this ? "

" I can hardly tell till I have seen myself," answered the horse. " But I feel sure I should look extremely magnificent ! "

King Jupiter waved his sceptre.

" You shall see yourself ! " said he. As he spoke, the earth seemed to shiver and move ; and up out of the floor of the palace rose a camel !

There it stood, this new and awful-looking beast ! Its neck, waving like a swan, carried a strange big head. Its wide chest was spread out above its long hairy legs. And in the very middle of its back rose an ugly hump. The horse saw it, and, breaking into a frothy sweat, trembled from head to foot with terror.

" *That* is what you would look like ! " thundered Jupiter. " Now do you still desire to have your shape improved, you most foolish horse ! "

" Oh, no, no ! " neighed the horse. " Please drive that horrible beast away ! I would not look like it for the world ! "

But Jupiter was gazing kindly at the camel.

" I have made a very useful, sensible beast, after all," said the King of Olympus. " I will send him to live in the desert, where no horse could exist for more than a few days. And I will

" There it stood, this new and awful-looking
beast ! "

keep him under my protection, just as I keep all the other animals of the world."

He patted the camel with his sceptre, and then turned to the horse.

"You shall remain the noble and beautiful creature you were born," said he. "But, in memory of your folly, you shall never get over your fear of the camel—that animal whom I made to show you the absurdity of your own ideas about improvements!"

And here you have the reason why horses have always been terrified by the sudden sight of camels from that day to this!

THE JAY AND THE NIGHTINGALE

DEEP in a green larch wood lived a family of jays, each of whom seemed to scream more harshly than his brothers. Never was there such a *"squ-ar-rrr-k"*—*"squ-ar-rrrrr-k!"* as when the party went a-hunting, which they generally did all together, taking it in turns to be sentinel on some high neighbouring tree. It was really a shockingly ugly noise that they produced, and, as they hid themselves as much as possible in their flight through the branches, its ugliness was not always made up for by a glimpse of their beautiful blue and fawn and black and white feathers.

The other birds in the wood did not like the jays at all, and with good reason. They had to be on the look-out, always, lest the jays should steal their eggs. But the jays did not care a rap however much they were disliked. They thought themselves lords of creation, and *" squ-ar-rrrr-k'd"* about their family grandeur at the very tops of their voices.

At last one young jay overheard some human

" Off the jay flew to the eagle, who sat on a high crag, staring at the sun."

P

beings talking about the beautiful song of the nightingale; saying that the nightingale was "the King of Song of the Woods." This annoyed young Master Jay very much indeed. Off he flew to the eagle, who sat on a high crag, staring at the sun.

"My Lord Eagle," said Master Jay, "I have just heard it said that the nightingale is called The 'King of Song of the Woods.' This I consider to be an insult to the jays, to whose family I belong! I therefore make a request that I shall be called the 'King of Song of the Woods.'"

The eagle fixed his piercing golden eyes upon the indignant young jay.

"I have no objection," said the bright-eyed beautiful lord of the birds calmly. "You may go back to your family and say I have named you the 'King of Song of the Woods,' if you like."

Away flew Master Jay again, hardly waiting to say "thank you." As soon as he reached the larch wood, on the edge of which the nightingales had made their home, he perched himself on a bough just above that snug little nest in the bramble thicket.

"*Squa-rr-k! Squ-a-a-a-rrrr-k!*" sang the jay, opening his beak as wide as it would go. "I am called the 'King of Song of the Woods!'

THE JAY AND THE NIGHTINGALE

Squa-rr-k! Let the nightingale be silent. He has lost his title. From to-day it belongs to me."

He went on screaming about his new title, till not only all the birds, but all the beasts of the wood came hurrying to see what was the matter. When they had listened for a minute to Master Jay's performance, they all hurried away as fast as they could, and the sound of their laughter bubbled through the trees like a brook.

"Listen to Master Jay," they called to each other. "Did ever you hear the like? He is shrieking out that he is, from to-day, to be named the 'King of Song of the Woods!'"

Master Jay heard their laughter die away in the distance. Deeply offended, he flew once more to the eagle, complaining bitterly.

"You, yourself, gave me the title of the 'King of Song of the Woods,' he screeched, circling round the crag where the eagle sat. "How is it, then, that all the birds and beasts of the forest are laughing at me?"

But the eagle remained quite calm and indifferent. He did not even take his bright eyes from the sun this time as he answered:

"My young friend, I certainly gave you the name of 'King of Song of the Woods' in answer to your request. But to *call* you so is one thing—to *make* you so is another!"

THE LITTLE PARTRIDGE'S STOLEN
EGGS

ON the shores of a great Eastern sea once lived a little bird called Teeteebha, with his wife, who was called Teeteebha too. They were pretty, plump birds, rather like red-legged partridges, which are fond of living near salt marshes and sandy flats. They picked and pecked among the shingle and sea-plants, and were very happy and contented. Still happier were they when Teeteebha, the wife, said to Teeteebha, the husband :

"My dear, the spring has come, and I must lay my eggs. Pray let us go inland and find a warm dry spot for our nest."

"Why should we go inland, little wife?" demanded the other bird. "Is not this place, where we get our daily food, good enough for you?"

"It is quite good enough, my dear," agreed Mrs. Teeteebha, "but, unfortunately, the great blue sea yonder sometimes flows right over it, and covers it with salt water!"

" Blue sea ! Salt water ! " cried Mr. Teeteebha in a little shrill croak. " Do you imagine that I am, then, so much less powerful than the ocean that I shall allow myself to be insulted in my own home ? Piff ! Paff ! Pouf ! "

And the little bird swelled himself out, and stretched himself up, till he looked like a fighting cock, glaring defiantly with his small bright eyes at the big, smooth, silent sea, which spread itself so majestically to the far horizon.

" Oh, my dear ! " cried Mrs. Teeteebha, half alarmed, half-laughing. " I know what a wonderful and clever partridge you are ! But there is a great deal of difference between the ocean and yourself."

" We shall see ! We shall see ! " snorted Mr. Teeteebha. " Anyway, you are my wife and must obey my orders. We will make our nest just there, under those rushes, and let the ocean interfere with our family arrangements if he dare ! "

So Mrs. Teeteebha, like a dutiful wife, helped her husband to make the nest under the rushes, and laid fourteen eggs, which she sat on in great pride and delight, looking forward to an early family of fourteen sons and daughters all the same age ! Now and then, however, she cast an anxious glance at the sea, hoping it would remain where it was, anyway, until the eggs were hatched. Mr. Teeteebha, in the meantime, strutted backwards and forwards in front of the waves, and every evening croaked a little croak of defiance to the powerful being who lay at the doors of his home.

But the Sea-King, as he guided his white-maned horses through the green plains of the water had heard the little partridge's foolish boast, and was angry. So, one night, this mighty monarch came driving up the beach, bringing all his waves along with him. And the waves carried off Mrs. Teeteebha's eggs, and placed them in a cave in the Sea-King's palace, under charge of the Princesses with the blue-green eyes and silver hair.

" O, lord of my heart," cried the poor little partridge to her husband. " What is to be done now ? The Sea-King, after all, was more powerful than we ! He has taken every one of my beautiful fourteen eggs ! "

Mr. Teeteebha shook his wet feathers in the moonlight. He would have shaken his fist, too, had he possessed one. As he did not he could only stretch his little claw threateningly in the direction of the dim and distant cave.

" My dear ! " he cried, " you must not despair ! Sometimes even a small thing, like a partridge, can get the better of a great thing, like the ocean ! I will call all the other birds together, and you will see what I can do ! "

So he called all the other birds together, and told them that the Sea-King had stolen Mrs. Teeteebha's fourteen eggs and hidden them in his palace below the waves. "And," he added, "I am too small a bird to recover them by myself! But I certainly intend to get them back! So I suggest that we go in a procession to the castle of King Eagle up in the Snow Mountain, and put the case in his hands. He will see justice done to us, for we are of his blood, though so much smaller in body and feebler in wing!"

The other birds agreed, and off they all set for the castle of King Eagle in the Snow Mountain —such a company of them, looking like a flying, fluttering rainbow, with their wings of crimson and gold, blue and green. Up the wooded sides of the great White Mountain they took their flight, and settled down as lightly as snowflakes upon the glistening carpet of frost and ice. There was the castle of King Eagle; and, higher up, was another wonderful palace, where a much mightier King lived, surrounded by stars and clouds, and waited upon by fairy beings who were even stronger and more beautiful than the Sea-King's daughters with the silver hair.

"Oh, great My Lord Eagle!" twittered and sang the chorus of little birds to the big bird in his robe of golden feathers, "we have come to ask your help. The Sea-King, down in the ocean yonder, has stolen Mrs. Teeteebha's fourteen beautiful eggs!"

"What made him do that!" asked King Eagle, gravely.

Mr. Teeteebha stood forward, in front of the others, and answered, proudly:

"He overheard me say that I refused to be insulted in my own home!" declared Mr. Teeteebha. "He took them to show that the ocean is stronger than a partridge! But, O great My Lord Eagle, what excuse is that?"

And all the other birds took up the chorus:

"Oh, great My Lord Eagle, what excuse is that?"

The Eagle frowned heavily. His bright big eyes surveyed Mr. Teeteebha from over his hooked beak.

"The Sea-King has taken a liberty!" he announced. "We will go all together to the great Emperor, Narayana, in the high palace up yonder, and he will take the matter into his own hands."

So the Eagle led Mr. Teeteebha and all the other birds up to Narayana, and told the story to the Emperor who lived in the palace among the stars. And Narayana frowned even more heavily than King Eagle had done.

"The ocean has taken a great liberty!"

thundered Narayana. "Yonder Sea-Monarch may be great and strong, but I cannot allow him to be cruel to the weak. My orders are "— and he thundered the words out so loudly that they travelled over mountain and valley down to the very bottom of the sea, and reached the ears of the Ocean-King where he sat on his coral throne—" my orders are that the eggs be given up immediately by the waves who took them, and put safely back in Mrs. Teeteebha's nest."

Then the Sea-King was dreadfully alarmed. It was one thing to steal tiny Mrs. Teeteebha's eggs, but quite another to have great Narayana thundering at him from the clouds above Snow Mountain ! . He fell into a great hurry to show the whole world that he had heard the order and meant to obey it. In less than five minutes he had risen from his cave to the top of the water ; and then all the birds and beasts who lived in the woods near that strange eastern coast saw a wonderful sight.

They saw the Sea-King driving his white horses quickly—ever so quickly—across the green plain of the ocean, with the silver-haired Princesses close to his chariot-wheels. In the folds of his robe lay Mrs. Teeteebha's treasures, and on his crown, in shining starry letters, were the words, " I hasten to obey the orders of Narayana and to restore to Mrs. Teeteebha her fourteen beautiful eggs ! "

Up the beach rolled the bright chariot, and still the crown showed Narayana's decree, sparkling in clearly-written words under the pale moon. Then the Sea-King's head was bent for a moment, crown and all. He was putting the eggs back, one by one, into the nest under the rushes, taking them carefully from his robe embroidered with diamonds and sapphires, emeralds and crystals, while two very small, very glad, very breathless little speckled brown birds looked on.

" *Ah-h-h !* " sighed Mrs. Teeteebha contentedly, as she settled down like a soft warm cushion on her eggs again, pushing and poking them into the right places under her breast. " Narayana is great, but not too great to look after the smallest and weakest of little birds ! "

" *Piff ! Paff ! Pouf !* " went Mr. Teeteebha proudly, once more strutting up and down *his* beach. " Didn't I tell you ? Narayana would not have me insulted in my own home ! "

But the Sea-King said nothing as he drove back to his dim and shining caves. The words written in his crown were enough.

THE MOON AND HER NEW DRESS

FOR months the snow had lain, white and sparkling, on the hilltops, and the ponds had been covered with ice. Then, all at once, the thaw came. Spring danced down the side of the mountain, and hung the rocks with curtains of beautiful saxifrages, and brought out whole bouquets of primroses and violets in the little corners that caught the early sun.

The evenings were calm and lovely, and clouds, as pretty as the flowers, clustered in the sky when the light died away. On one of these fair evenings up through the clouds climbed the little new moon, dressed in the pale silver frock that she had worn all the winter, and all last summer and autumn as well.

She looked down towards the earth, and saw that everything on it was clothed in a delicate new gown. The almond-trees shook their pink skirts gracefully, and the elms drew their green scarves round their shoulders. So what should the little new moon do but start a-weeping where she hung in the clear evening sky, and asking the stars and the winds why she was not allowed a new frock like everybody else?

The stars and winds did their best to comfort her, but without success. Then, hearing her little daughter's sobs, who should come floating up from the sea, but the mother of the moon herself!

What the mother of the moon was like nobody could describe to you, except the old people who told this story to their children more than two thousand years ago. But we can very well guess that she had eyes that could see to the other end of nowhere, and that the memory of the sunlight hung about her hair.

She hurried to the side of the little new moon and asked what was the matter. And the little silver lady explained through her tears that she wanted a new dress—a dress that must be made in the height of the spring fashion. The mother of the moon promised to do her best for her daughter, and said that she would start making the dress immediately, and come the very next night to try it on.

She went away, and the little new moon shone with all her might, dreaming about the grand new dress. She wondered if it would be made of pearly cloud-stuff, and most likely she hoped that it would be trimmed with stars.

At cock-crow she slipped silently home, but,

the next evening, she climbed the sky in great excitement, and waited for her wonderful gown.

Then the mother of the moon came along with her daughter's frock, and slipped it over the new moon's head. But, behold, it would not fit! It was a great deal too small round the waist.

"Oh, dear! oh, dear!" wailed the little moon, "you have cut it out all wrong!"

"Indeed, I have not," answered her mother angrily. "It is you who are to blame! You have grown bigger in the night!"

"Then take it home and let it out!" snapped the little new moon pettishly. And she pulled her pretty silver shoulders out of the frock, and pushed it away, with a pout.

The mother of the moon shook her head. But, all the same, she took the frock away, and brought it back the next evening, duly let out.

The new moon was waiting among the stars, and her kind mother again popped the frock over her daughter's bright hair. But a second time it would not meet round the waist.

"You have cut it out wrong again!" cried the little new moon in a temper. "It doesn't fit."

"It is not likely to!" answered the mother, herself quite angry. "You're even bigger than you were yesterday!"

THE MOON AND HER NEW DRESS

" Nonsense ! " wailed the new moon. " Oh, please take it home, dear mother, and try again ! "

So, a third time, her patient mother let out the frock, and added a big piece to the hem. Then, once more, she carried it up to the sky to see if it would fit.

The little new moon was silent and rather upset. As she had climbed the sky she had suspected herself that her waist was even bigger than before. And, sure enough, when the frock was put over her head, the hooks and eyes were farther apart than ever.

" Oh, take it away ! " cried the new moon. " I'm not a baby now ! I'm growing up as fast as I can ! If I can't have a dress fit for a grown-up lady, it's a pity ! "

She never even thanked her mother for her trouble, but looked down sulkily at her reflection in a lake below. However, the mother of the moon determined to try again. For a whole fortnight, she went on letting out the gown ; but at the end of the two weeks the new moon was a perfect ball round the middle, ever so many times bigger than she had been at first.

Then, to her mother's delight, she began all at once to grow smaller.

" Now I can fit her ! " said her mother joyfully. And she got a fresh piece of stuff, and began all over again. But, this time, the frock hung on the moon like a sack. It was much too big.

And so, for another week or two, the patient mother, instead of letting out the moon's frock, had to be taking it in! Until, at last, she gave up the struggle to fit the moon with a new gown. And that is the reason why, year in, year out, the moon never changes her silver colour, though, as all of you know, she is for ever changing her size.

THE VAIN JACKDAW

ONCE upon a time the Emperor of All the Animals in the World thought that the Bird-People would be the better off for a Vassal-King of their own. So he sent out notices far and wide, telling the birds to present themselves before his throne ; and saying that, when he had looked them well over, he would choose the most beautiful among them to reign over the rest.

East and west and south and north went his messengers with the summons. They went to the humming-birds that sip the flower-sweets, and to the great eagles that sweep over the tops of the highest rockiest hills—to the owls, and the ostriches, the peacocks, the penguins, and the pigeons. And all the birds began to preen their feathers, and cock their pretty heads, in readiness for the great day.

The jackdaw, however, was very discontented. He knew that he was an ugly sort of bird, and he saw no chance of being chosen as King. However, he hit on what seemed to him to be a very happy idea. What do you think he did ?

He went hunting over the fields and through the woods for the feathers that the other birds had dropped. And, when he had collected as many as he could find, he dressed himself up in them ! There was every kind of feather you can think of, but perhaps most beautiful of all were the long plumes, green and blue and gold, that had fallen from the peacocks' tails. Then, when the great day came, he stuck these stolen feathers all over his body in what he thought was a very striking design, and set out for the palace of the Emperor, managing his finery with some difficulty, and rather nervous lest any of it should blow off.

What a procession of lovely birds there was before the Emperor's throne ! It was a regular Court day in Birdland. One after another the pretty things arrived at the palace, some of them hopping or running up the paths, others alighting delicately from the sky. Such a twittering and singing and chirping had never been heard before, and will certainly never be heard again. And, one by one, the birds all passed in front of the Emperor, while he examined them carefully, and tried to make up his mind which was the most beautiful.

At last he called the jackdaw to come and stand by the side of the throne. Proud as the

" Then came all the other birds whom the jackdaw had robbed of their pretty feathers."

peacock, whose stolen feathers were trailing behind him, the jackdaw marched up and stood there for every other bird to stare at. Then the Emperor told his herald to blow a trumpet, and to declare that the jackdaw, in his wonderful dress of feathers, was the finest inhabitant of Birdland, and was to be crowned its King.

This was too much for the rest of the birds. A great commotion rose among them, and out dashed a pair of pigeons and tore their pretty feathers from the jackdaw's breast, followed by a screaming jay, who claimed the blue patch lost, long ago, from his wing. Then came all the others whom the jackdaw had robbed. Last of all, the peacock himself marched up, his great beautiful tail raised in anger, making a shining frame for his gleaming sapphire head. He seized the mock tail of the robber and threw it on the ground at the Emperor's feet. And there, all his fine feathers gone, stood the ugly jackdaw, black and foolish-looking, and making disgusted little croaking noises under his breath!

So, instead of being made King, he was driven away in disgrace, while the other birds called and chirped and twittered after him:

"Fine feathers don't make fine birds!"

"Fine feathers never *have* made fine birds!"

"Fine feathers never *will* make fine birds!"

"*Shoo!* Shoo! SHOO!"

THE ACORN AND THE VEGETABLE MARROW

A GARDENER who spent all his days sowing and planting, plucking and pruning, had got into a habit of thinking he knew the best way to do everything that could be done among vegetables, trees, and flowers. He was not alone in this belief. It is one that a good many gardeners have had, ever since the first rose-bush was set in the first rose-bed. But he was really a terribly conceited fellow, and began at last to imagine that, if he only had the opportunity, he could improve on the beautiful and wonderful plan of creation itself.

"These foolish vegetable marrows now!" he thought one day as he tied them up with string to prevent them from breaking their soft, long stalks. "Why in the world should they grow in such an absurd fashion? If I had my way they should grow on an oak! What a fine sight that would be! An oak laden with hundreds of vegetable marrows instead of acorns! Strange, very strange, that such a plan is not carried out by Nature!"

" ' If that had been a marrow instead of an acorn,' said the gardener, ' it would certainly have killed me ! ' "

ACORN AND THE VEGETABLE MARROW

He sat down under a neighbouring oak tree to eat his dinner, and all the time kept wondering why vegetable marrows did not grow on its boughs! They would be so much grander and more suitable than the little acorns in their tiny rough cups. While he was grumbling to himself in this conceited way he fell fast asleep, leaning back against the trunk of the tree, with his face turned up to its branches.

Flop! Flop! Flip! Down fell one of the acorns on his nose, with such a bang that it woke him immediately. He started up, wondering what in the world could have hit him in this unexpected manner. In a moment he perceived that his nose had been struck by a falling acorn, struck so smartly that it had begun to bleed a little.

" Goodness, gracious me ! " said the gardener with horror, dabbing his nose with his big red handkerchief, " what a blessing my idea about oak trees and vegetable marrows *was* an idea, and not a reality ! If that had been a marrow instead of an acorn it would certainly have killed me ! I see that there is a good deal of sense in the way Nature docs things after all."

From that day onwards, he was less conceited.

THE ASS DRESSED IN A TIGER'S SKIN

IN an old, old Indian city lived a dyer who was so cunning that he went by the name of "Artful." He was a bit of a rogue in more than one way, and would always rather cheat people than do honest business with them. Perhaps he had dyed too many stuffs in too many different colours to be really quite sure what was black and what white!

As well as being cunning, he was both greedy and cruel. He owned a donkey, which he over-worked and under-fed. At last the poor donkey, worn out with carrying loads that were much too heavy, fell so ill that he could carry no more. He was thinner than any donkey in the district, and his master was really afraid that, if he did not get some good food, he would die.

The question was how to buy cheap food for the donkey—in fact, how to get hay or corn without paying anything at all. The dyer—whom we will call Vilasa, as that is the Indian word for Artful—thought the matter over, and

THE ASS IN A TIGER'S SKIN

finally hit upon what he considered an excellent plan.

He went to the bazaar and bought a tiger skin, large and glossy, in stripes of yellow and black. The tail still hung upon it; the legs and feet and claws; and the head was quite perfect, with its upright cat-like ears and long teeth. Carrying this fine skin home with him, he went to the donkey, where it drooped feebly in a corner of the yard. Vilasa tied the skin carefully all round the donkey, so that you could see nothing but the fine glossy stripes of the tiger, and nothing at all of the donkey's back, and legs, and head.

When this was safely and cleverly finished, the dyer waited for the sun to set and the moon to rise. Then he took a bridle and a stick, and led the donkey out of the city towards the open plain, where the corn and rice-fields lay. And surely the moon has rarely looked on a stranger sight than that of Vilasa leading along the hobbling old donkey, dressed up in the skin of the dead and gone tiger.

Presently, the man came to a specially fine field, full of ripe waving heads of grain. Into the middle of the field Vilasa pulled and pushed his tired beast. The donkey immediately lay down and began to eat all the corn he could reach without moving; while Vilasa went home to get on with his business of dyeing yellow things purple, and white things scarlet and blue.

Morning broke, and the reapers came along with their sickles to cut the field of grain. What was their dismay to see the glossy stripes and pricked ears of a tiger right in the middle of the field! One and all turned and ran for their lives. So did the owner of the field, and his wife, and his sons, and his daughters, and everybody else who came along and caught sight of what they thought was a tiger stretched out among the corn.

This went on for some few days, and the donkey got so plump that, while he had at first lain down for weariness, he now did so for fatness. But he was very pleased with his present life. He had a whole field of delicious grain to munch, and whoever peeped over the corn-stalks and caught sight of him immediately took to his heels and ran away.

There was, however, one man braver than the rest, whose business it was to visit the different fields of corn, and see how much money each crop was likely to be worth. He was a cunning man, quite as cunning as Vilasa. One day he watched the supposed tiger for a long time from a safe distance—the top of a tree, to be on the sure side—then he went home, and what do you think he did?

THE ASS IN A TIGER'S SKIN

It was something as clever and artful as Vilasa had done; in fact, more so.

He went to the bazaar, bought a donkey's skin, and dressed himself up in it very carefully indeed. Then he took his bow and arrows and set out for the corn-field. When he got there, he stooped among the grain, so that only his hairy back could be seen, with his long ears waving above the corn. Then, clutching his bow and arrows firmly—for in spite of his suspicions, it might have been a real tiger, after all—he made his way through the slim yellow stalks towards the other animal in the middle of the field.

What an odd affair it must have been! There was the donkey in the tiger skin, and the man in the donkey skin, each peeping at the other over the cornstalks. But the donkey, now as plump as plump could be, was a foolish creature, after all. He gave a loud bray of delight, tossed his head, and trotted gaily off to meet the other. "For," said he to himself, " Hee-haw! Hee-haw! Here is a handsome friend—quite likely a lady-friend—come to join me in my comfortable life among the corn. Hee-haw! "

Poor donkey! No sooner had he stretched out his funny head, all tied up in the tiger skin, to rub noses with the new donkey, than up rose the strange animal on its hind-legs, in a way no true ass had ever been known to do. Then over the real donkey's head were flung bit and bridle, and away he was dragged through the cornfield by the man with the bow and arrows. And all the people who had been so frightened came together on the path beyond crying out to each other :

" Come and see! Oh, do come and see! What we thought was a savage and terrible wild beast is only Vilasa's old donkey as full of our corn as a drum is full of air! Aha! an ass in a tiger skin is a clever thing, but a man in an ass's skin is a hundred thousand times cleverer!"

THE DOG AND THE SHADOW

A LARGE dog had stolen a delicious piece of bony beef from the kitchen, and was running off with it as fast as he could, when he came to a stream bridged by a plank. As he trotted across the plank, suddenly he saw a very strange thing. Down in the clear quiet water was another dog, with another piece of beef!

" Ho ! " said Master Doggie to himself, " What's this ! A dog with a piece of beef, down there ! And a much bigger piece than mine is ! I'll take it from him ! "

He opened his mouth to seize the beef from the dog in the water—when lo ! down plopped his own dinner with a loud splash ! The ripples cleared, and there, staring up out of the water, was the dog, with jaws as empty as his own !

It had been his shadow that he had seen all the time—and the shadow, too, of his piece of beef !

THE MAN AND THE LION

A MAN and a lion were once taking a walk together through a beautiful wood. A strange couple they must have looked as they strolled side by side under the shadows, and how amazed the birds and beasts must have been to see them! They talked quite amiably for a time, but by and by the man began to boast of his strength and muscle, which made the lion answer that although men might be strong, lions were certainly stronger. He must have been a kind sort of lion not to prove his words by eating the man up on the spot. However, he did not even bare his teeth, except when he opened his mouth a little wider than usual in his earnestness.

Though this strange couple did not exactly quarrel, they argued very hotly indeed. At last they came to a clearing in the forest, and there —probably in memory of some great hunt— stood a wonderful statue of a lion which was being strangled by a tall, strong man. The man

" ' See that statue,' cried the man, ' and then
admit that you are beaten in our argument !
Actually a statue has been carved and set
up to show that a man *is* stronger than a
lion ! ' "

" ' What a pity,' remarked the beast, ' that
lions were never taught to carve ! ' "

who walked by the lion's side gave an exclamation of triumph.

"See that statue," he cried, "and then admit that you are beaten in our argument! There is the proof of what I have been saying! Actually a statue has been carved and set up to show that a man *is* stronger than a lion!"

The lion walked up to the statue, and paced slowly round it, staring at it thoughtfully. Then he strolled back to the man, tossing his mane in contempt. His golden-brown eyes looked very scornful.

"Ah!" said he, with a wise wag of his tawny head, "that statue is nothing to go by—nothing at all! It was carved by a *man*! Now if I—I, or any other lion—had only learnt how to handle a chisel, you would have seen quite a different sort of statue set up among the ferns at the crossways!"

"Indeed!" answered the man. "Pray what should I have seen?"

"Oh! just the other side of the story!" remarked the lion, brushing his whiskers with his great paw. "A man being strangled by a lion, that's all! What a pity it is that lions were never taught to carve!"

THE FOX AND THE ROOK

ONE beautiful summer evening an army of rooks were flying across the blue sky, cawing at the top of their voices. All day they had been digging in the grass for cock-chafer grubs, and now they were going home to their tents of leaves and twigs high in the tree-tops, ready for their night's sleep. There were old birds, and middle-aged birds, some of them getting a little grey about the beak, and very young, sprightly birds, with feathers as black as jet. These young birds had only been hatched in the Spring, but they could fly as fast and as far as their parents, and caw quite as loudly, though perhaps with a little less sense.

Among them was a young rook who was so pleased with her bright eyes and brand new wings that she was keeping rather away from the others, and flapping home all by herself. She was a terribly conceited little rook, ever on the look out for admiration. Also, she was very greedy. So her eyes sparkled with pleasure when, flying past the open window of a house, she

" For, when the simpering silly rook opened her beak to sing, the cold beef fell with a little soft plop into the bracken."

R

THE FOX AND THE ROOK

caught sight of a table spread with a delicious-looking supper. Down on to the sill swept my lady crow, swooped in through the casement, snatched up a large slice of cold beef, and flew out again as fast as her wings could carry her. Quite breathless with hurry—and also with the weight of the cold beef—she settled on a big fir tree to rest for a few minutes, while the branch on which she had perched swayed and shook its pretty green needles under the sudden burden.

As she sat there, holding very firmly on to the beef, the dying sunshine fell upon something lithe and ruddy down among the plumy bracken at the foot of the tree. Out from under a prickly gorse bush slipped a fox, silent as a shadow, but bright and red-golden in the evening light. He was setting out on his night's hunting, and was very hungry. So when he looked up at the rook, his mouth positively watered at the sight of the delicious cold beef.

The rook cocked her head to one side, and glanced down upon the fox rather scornfully. In spite of his handsome brush, which trailed with such grace behind him when he came out from the bushes, she thought him a vulgar fellow at best. She had no idea that he was the cleverest among all the animals of the forest, infinitely cleverer than she was herself. And cunning Mr. Fox, the moment he saw the slice of roast meat, made up his mind that he would have it for his supper.

So down he squatted at the root of the tree, brushed his whiskers, and began to make eyes at the rook. Then he spoke, in a voice which trembled with admiration.

"What lovely creature is it that I see seated upon the tree overhead? Out of what fairylike nest did those delicate wings take their first flight? Never have I seen a bird like this one! The very swans would hide their heads under the water for shame if they beheld her beauty! How bright are her eyes! And her complexion—why, it is fairer than the lilies, and pinker and downier than a sunripe peach! Her toes, too! How adorably they are pointed! She looks as if she could dance as exquisitely as she flies!"

The fox paused for breath. Also to think of a few more compliments. The rook began to simper, and sidle, and cock her head from side to side. But she took very good care to hold tightly on to the beef!

Then the fox licked his lips and began again.

"I believe that this wonderful creature is the beautiful young rook of whom I have so often heard! If so, then is it true that her face and figure are rather belied by her voice? I am told that she makes strange noises when she opens her beak, but I do not believe it! An exquisite being such as she must be able to sing more sweetly than the nightingale. Oh, what would I not give to hear that melting song— perhaps even to join in the notes, until all the neighbourhood gathered together to listen to the melody of our duet!"

By this time the conceited young rook had entirely lost her head, so delighted was she with the fox's admiration. She had quite changed her mind about his vulgarity, and thought him a marvellously wise and elegant beast. When she heard his last words she could not remain silent any longer. She must really show him that her voice was as fine as her face and her form. Forgetting all about the slice of cold roast beef, she opened her beak as wide as it would go and began to sing.

"*Caw! Caw! Caw!*" croaked the little black rook, making the ugliest noise you ever heard in your life. And "*Woof!*" went the fox at the root of the tree. But he only gave one "*Woof!*" and this was a great bark of excitement. For, when the simpering silly rook opened her beak to sing, the cold beef fell with a little soft plop into the bracken, and the fox instantly snatched it up and galloped away with it.

"Caw! Caw! Caw!" screamed the rook. "You wicked red thief! Give me back my cold beef! Caw! Caw! Caw!"

But she cawed in vain, her eyes sparkling with anger, and her tiny red tongue showing inside her open yellow beak. The fox only galloped away the faster. And, as he went, he called back over his shoulder, in rather muffled tones, for *he* was not going to lose his hold of the beef:

" I won't give any opinion on your voice, Miss Rook, but I certainly don't think much of your

The Wonder Books

Each Crown 4to, Picture Boards. Also Cloth. 8 Colour Plates in each. 256 Pages. Over 300 Illustrations.

THESE popular and well-known gift books are appropriate to every season of the year and to every occasion—birthdays, prize-givings, Christmas, etc. They are constantly revised and brought up to date, and contain much that is of interest not only to young people but to their elders.

The Wonder Book of

Would You Believe It?

WONDERFUL—almost unbelievable—things that are true. A fascinating volume.

The Wonder Book of **Daring Deeds**

TRUE Stories of Heroism and Adventure. The book describes the exploits of some of those whose names are bywords throughout the world. The stories are brightly written and delightfully illustrated, and, what is more—they are all true !

The Wonder Book of **Machinery**

THIS "Machine Age" calls for a Wonder Book. Here it is, revealing to modern boys and girls many of the marvels of present-day machinery.

The Wonder **Book of Electricity**

THIS is indeed an electric age. In addition to describing "everyday" things, this fascinating book tells us of many wonders now accomplished by electricity.

The Wonder **Book of Railways**

is a great favourite with all boys and girls who are "keen" on railways. The interest is not confined to Great Britain, for there are pictures and articles concerning railways in all countries.

The Wonder **Book of Ships**

ALL about the great liners and other vessels of the Merchant Navy, with hundreds of pictures that make an instant appeal to all who love the sea.

WARD, LOCK & CO., LIMITED, LONDON, E.C.4